MOON GARDEN

After recovering from a nervous breakdown, Ellen comes to her aunt Minna's Southern mansion to regain her strength, but strange events begin to haunt her. She glimpses people in various places, only to be told by those people that they had never been there; when they also deny the reality of other things Ellen claims to have seen, she is forced to consider whether her illness is returning to poison her thoughts. Only when a woman she has seen is found murdered, does Ellen finally realise the terrifying truth . . .

V. J. BANIS

MOON GARDEN

Complete and Unabridged

LINFORD
Leicester

First published in Great Britain

First Linford Edition
published 2014

A catalogue record for this book is available
from the British Library.

ISBN 978–1–4448–2158–1

Published by
F. A. Thorpe (Publishing)
Anstey, Leicestershire

Set by Words & Graphics Ltd.
Anstey, Leicestershire
Printed and bound in Great Britain by
T. J. International Ltd., Padstow, Cornwall

This book is printed on acid-free paper

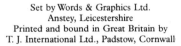

1

Fire!

Hot and cold played in alternating waves over her bare arms — the cold of the night air, the rush of heat from the flames. The glow gave her face, which would have been ashen in any other light, a ghastly pallor. Her eyes were unearthly wide, filled to the brim with the flickering horror before her.

Someone brushed rudely against her, almost knocking her off balance. A fireman went by, rushing on some errand that would be too late.

Too late to save the house. Too late to save the man trapped inside. Too late . . .

One of the chimneys collapsed, falling through what remained of the roof. A volcanic eruption of smoke and ash and fire burst upward.

Then, as if her entire soul weren't already blackened into ash, as if she hadn't already known her last moment of inner peace, as if she hadn't already condemned herself to the eternal fires of hell — as she stood shivering in the cold of the night, there came from within the inferno that terrible scream. The cry of a man as his life is wrested from him.

It went on and on. She heard it even through the blackness that enveloped her with would-be mercy. She heard it while the doctors probed and questioned.

She embroidered little flowers on useless doilies, and heard that scream.

She took soothing walks with the kindly nurse, and the trees screamed.

She slept the man-made sleep of sedation. Even in her sleep, she heard the scream.

With it, crashing through her mind over and over and over, was that one awful thought.

I killed him. I killed my father.

★   ★   ★

The sky was so very blue, the air so very fresh. Of course it was the same sky and the same air that she had been seeing and breathing when she was at Lawndale. But they seemed changed when you are free, seeing them without walls about you, with no chaperoning nurse close at hand to report your every look and action to the psychiatrists.

True, they were a little frightening too. She waited for the traffic light to change. A tall girl in a stunning outfit stepped impatiently off the curb and started across, dodging cars. Ellen watched her, envying her boldness, her easy self-confidence, but she did not emulate her. She waited until the light changed and the others had started across before she moved from the curb.

Cincinnati had completed its renovation of the square since she had been away — she thought of it that way, as 'away' and not 'in a mental hospital.' In its center was the old fountain, still handsome despite the stark modernity of its new setting.

At the far corner she paused while waiting for the light, and looked back. She would probably not have noticed the young man had he not been watching her so intently he ran right into a woman with her arms full of packages.

The packages went everywhere. Ellen Miles watched the two of them scrambling for the packages, the woman looking quite put out, the young man, in his nondescript clothes, obviously embarrassed.

Someone jostled her. The light had changed and she crossed the street. On the opposite side she looked back once more. The woman was still there, looking over her packages. The young man was gone.

Because it was such a lovely day, and her first day in a long time that she could be anywhere really by herself, and because a young man had just been watching with such keen interest as she crossed the square, she laughed aloud.

The laugh was short-lived. She put a hand to her mouth to hide it and thought, if they see me laughing out loud to myself, they'll send me back. She hurried on, forgetting all about the young man.

She approached the restaurant table where her mother sat waiting and realized she was late. Mrs. Miles watched her daughter make her way through the maze of tables.

'I was beginning to worry,' she began in a scolding tone.

'I'm only five minutes late.'

'But you were alone . . . '

'I'd have to be some time,' Ellen said, but in a kindly tone. She really hadn't meant to make her mother worry. She had simply been enjoying herself so much that she hadn't watched the time. At Lawndale, everyone had watched the time for her, had told her when to come and when to go, when to eat and sleep, and sometimes when to dream. She would have to readjust to the idea of time.

'Did you find everything you wanted?' Mrs. Miles asked when the waitress had come and gone.

'Pretty much so. Anyway, I suppose Savannah has plenty of stores of its own.'

'It's a very lovely city,' Mrs. Miles said, with altogether too much enthusiasm. It was her idea that Ellen should go to Savannah, where there would not be so much to remind her of what had happened. She would have been offended if anyone had suggested too that Ellen served to remind her of things she would be happier forgetting, or that she was not quite comfortable in the presence of a daughter who had suffered a nervous breakdown.

'Tell me about Savannah,' Ellen said aloud, partly because it was a safe topic for conversation.

'I don't remember a good deal, to tell the truth,' Mrs. Miles said, needlessly stirring a tall glass of iced tea. 'I was there twice. Once when I married Fred. That was during the war. And the second time when you were about three. I don't suppose you remember anything?'

Ellen shook her head. 'No. Unless . . . there is something, but I'm not even sure that it's real, or just some piece of childish nonsense.'

'What's that?'

'A moon garden. I don't even know what it means, it's just a phrase that popped into my head. Maybe I read it somewhere.'

'But there *is* a moon garden. Oh dear.'

Mrs. Miles looked truly anguished now. 'It's an ugly old story. And it's supposed to be haunted.'

So am I, Ellen thought. 'I wouldn't worry about that,' she said aloud. 'It sounds very romantic, anyway. A crumbling southern mansion — it is crumbling, isn't it? A moon garden, whatever exactly that is. And ghosts on top of everything. Darling, it ought to be enough to take anyone's mind off of almost anything.'

'Ellen, dear, maybe you oughtn't to go after all.' Mrs. Miles said. 'Aunt Minna is a bit eccentric. She always was, and it's been so long since I've really seen her or talked to her. Heaven only knows, by this time she might be completely crazy . . . '

She dropped her spoon, spilling soup and causing a number of heads to turn in their direction.

Ellen had a mischievous impulse to say, 'We ought to be really good company for one another.' But her mother looked so close to crying that she suppressed the urge, and pretended she hadn't even caught that slip of the tongue. 'Tell me about the moon garden. It sounds quite fascinating.'

'Ellen, about your father . . . '

'No,' Ellen said, emphatically. 'That's the past. He's gone.' She hesitated a moment, and said again, 'Tell me about the moon garden.'

★   ★   ★

Three men waited in a hotel room not far away. Two of them were seated in big armchairs, but they were not relaxed.

The third man was their superior, many times removed. He could afford to be relaxed in their company, and he was. He was tall and portly. There was something almost uncouth in his heavy and massive build, something in the slow way he moved that suggested a physical inertia. But he had what used to be called a masterful brow, and his eyes, deep set and the color of steel, were alert.

He went once or twice to the window and pulled the curtains a little aside to look out.

A knock sounded at the door. One of the seated men sprang up with an athletic quickness and went to the door. The second man remained seated, but his hand had gone inside his sport coat.

Whispered words were exchanged at the door. The shoulders of the man inside relaxed visibly, and he stepped aside briefly to allow someone to enter.

The newcomer was a young man, a little more than five feet ten inches in height, and slender, and he moved with the sort of controlled grace that evidenced perfect physical training. He was blond and his eyes were pale blue.

The man who had opened the door introduced him curtly to the man at the window. 'Ken Parker, Walt Nielsen.' They shook hands. Both grips were strong. Parker looked as relaxed as Nielsen.

'You've checked out this girl?' Nielsen asked.

'Yes. There's no doubt she's really a relative. A niece, on her father's side. I've made up a full report.' He took an envelope from his pocket and handed it to Nielsen. Nielsen tossed it to one of the other men, who opened it and began to read silently.

'Of course,' Nielsen said, 'we'll want to be sure it's the same girl who shows up in Savannah.'

'I'll be there when she arrives,' Parker said. He paused for a moment. 'There's one thing. I think she saw me. That is, actually took a look at me. I was following her across Fountain Square, and a woman with her arms full of packages ran into me. As luck would have it, the girl chose just that moment to glance back.'

'Did she see your face?'

'Not for more than a second. I turned my back on her fast, and got away as quickly as I could. I don't think she'll recognize me.'

'We'll risk it. What kind of a girl is she, this niece?'

Parker took a few seconds to consider his answer. He knew what Nielsen wanted — not the sort of details included in the report. He wanted a label, something that would tell him where to file this girl in his mind.

'Fragile,' Parker said finally. 'Easily broken.'

Nielsen was pleased. 'Easily broken,' he repeated. He nodded his head, sending little rippling waves through a succession of chins. 'Good,' he muttered. 'Good.'

2

She hadn't killed him, of course, her father. That was the guilt talking, as the doctors had explained to her. Yes, she had wished him dead, even as she loved him — that cruel, domineering man who had kept her very nearly a prisoner all her young life. The fire, though, had been his own doing, a drunken man's careless accident. She had learned not to blame herself for that. For any of it, really. He had loved her, had wanted her, at least. Perhaps his wanting had not been healthy, perhaps not even sane. It couldn't matter. Whatever had or hadn't been, she was free now.

Ellen knew she was not wanted at Aunt Minna's. She had been even more strongly not wanted with the various other relatives. Everyone had flatly refused, and then when it seemed that no one would take her in, Minna Miles had relented.

Well, it was something, knowing you weren't really wanted. But it had been important that she get away. Dr. Hanson had thought so too, and she had been willing to swallow a little pride. She had in mind that she would quickly establish a working relationship with her aunt. She would be as little trouble as possible. When Aunt Minna saw that she wasn't going to be a nuisance, that she was content to occupy herself and let her aunt do the same, everything would be all right. That, at any rate, was what she hoped for.

The plane was swooping downward and outside the window the blue faded into gray, and finally became concrete, rushing by, slowing, stopping altogether. They were at the terminal. She unfastened the seatbelt that she had kept tight across her throughout the flight, and let the stream of passengers carry her inside.

Aunt Minna had said she would be met. She had simply taken for granted that they would somehow recognize and find her, but when she had waited for some time she began to wonder if there had been a mix-up.

When she caught herself thinking wistfully of the sense of security she had known in Lawndale, she shook herself angrily and went to the doors that led outside. There were taxis there, and she got into one, giving the driver her aunt's address. This, she thought as the cab sped away, was what she should have done anyway.

★　★　★

The Terrace, where Aunt Minna lived, was no longer a fashionable part of town. It had once been the outskirts, but had since been swallowed up by a spreading industrial section. They passed a large bottling plant, and an open park, and at last a street of once lovely houses, decorated with much ironwork.

They were near the river, although Ellen was a little confused as to its exact location. She thought the Terrace looked quite romantically lovely, if a bit unkempt.

Number fourteen was the end house

with the thick columns. She had no idea how old it was, but she guessed it had stood there well over a century, perhaps closer to two centuries. Sadly, it was showing its age now. The paint was beginning to peel. The steps up to the front door sagged; a shutter at a window had a slightly lopsided tilt.

She paid the cabdriver, and waited on the sidewalk until he had driven out of sight. She was putting off the moment of going up the steps to number fourteen.

When the cab had completely vanished, she turned toward the house. A light glinted in her eyes, though the sun was to her right and behind her. She looked down and saw a little sliver of light dancing on the pavement and knew at once what it was. She remembered as a little girl playing with a mirror and the sun. This was the same sort of light. She looked around, but there were no children in sight.

Then she looked up. Above, protruding from a second floor window, was the end of a telescope, the sun reflecting from its lens. As she looked up, it disappeared inside.

She went up the steps and rang the bell. A young woman in a maid's uniform opened the door a crack and asked, 'What do you want?'

'Miss Miles, to see Miss Miles,' Ellen said, which seemed to confuse the girl, who only stood, studying her doubtfully. While she was trying to make up her mind what to say in reply, Ellen heard a sound within. She looked past the maid, into the cool, dark interior, and saw a woman at the top of the stairs. She was tall and at that precise moment she was adjusting on her head a preposterous feather hat.

Satisfied the hat was right, she descended the stairs majestically. The hallway, so vast a moment before, seemed actually to shrink in size.

'Why isn't Mrs. Bondage answering the door?' she demanded of the servant, who seemed to have shrunk somewhat too.

'She's in the basement, ma'am,' the young woman said almost in a whisper, 'having her astrology read.'

The feathered lady said, 'Really?' as if this were the most incredible piece of news she had ever been given. She took a moment to digest it, and then said, 'That will do, Bertha.'

Bertha was glad to be dismissed. She threw a last, curious look at Ellen, and scurried away, leaving Ellen to the mercy of her wondrous hostess.

The older woman threw the massive front door wider, and smiled. 'Good afternoon,' she said in a voice like sorghum. 'What can I do for you?'

Ellen took a deep breath and said, 'I'm your niece, Ellen Miles. You are my aunt Minna, aren't you?'

The smile faded. 'Oh no,' she said, 'no indeed, that's quite impossible. My niece is to arrive tomorrow, by airplane. I've made arrangements to have her met.'

Ellen looked a little disconcerted in the face of this. 'But I am here,' she said almost apologetically. 'And I am your niece.'

Minna took a step closer, and leaned forward a little. She had not worn her glasses down. What she saw was a pretty face, young, frightened-looking, but with a nice upward tilt to the chin.

'Yes,' she said, sounding oddly disappointed. 'You look like your mother. Our side of the family was better-looking. You said in your letter you would be arriving tomorrow.'

'I said today. The eighteenth. This is the eighteenth.'

'I know the date. I'm not a fool. You said the nineteenth. Oh, never mind, you're here. You may as well know, I didn't want you to come.'

Ellen looked embarrassed. 'I got that impression.' She had her hands clasped in front of her again. She looked like a little girl being scolded.

'I suggested your mother write to her family.' Aunt Minna regarded her niece as she might some tropical bird, or a peculiar flower that had just been delivered to her door. But although her conversation was rude, there was an unmistakable gleam of mischief in her eyes, and something like a toss of the head that set the feathers of her hat dancing in the sun.

'I believe my mother did write them. I don't know exactly what was said, but since I am here, and not there, it must be a bit obvious, don't you think?'

The grin came back to the old face. Minna knew that the others had refused to take child in. When she had learned of this she had changed her mind, and had extended her own somewhat reluctant invitation. She loathed that other branch of the family, so much so that she had an automatic inclination toward anyone they had rejected. It had been as simple as that.

She saw now, however, that her niece had courage. She liked that, and warmed to her at once.

'Your mother's people are Yankees. They made glue out of fish.' She extended her hand in a hospitable gesture. 'Come in, come in. We'll have tea. You must be exhausted after your journey. I traveled to Cincinnati once. I've forgotten how many days it took. I couldn't get grits anywhere.'

Ellen was not in the habit of tea in the afternoon but one was reluctant to decline this woman's suggestions, and she allowed herself to be wafted by sheer force of character up the stairs and into a sitting room, where she was stationed on a gilt settee.

The trip, the flying, to which she was unaccustomed, the crowds of people . . . it had all been fun but wearying. She would have liked to sink into a comfortable deep chair, or better still, to lie down somewhere, but she kept her shoulders back and sat solidly on the hard settee. Something about her aunt demanded that she keep her shoulders back. What a contrast to her mother's softness, sometimes so hard to get hold of.

Tea was already laid on a lace cloth atop a highly polished table, but it was clear that Aunt Minna had already had hers. She put a finger to the little silver teapot, found it cold, and with a gesture of indignation, yanked at a velvet rope by the door.

A maid, not Bertha but another middle-aged one, appeared quickly. She was sent off with orders to bring a fresh pot of tea. This, Ellen decided, was Mrs.

Bondage. She looked flustered and Ellen hoped that her astrologer had foretold a fortune that was good enough to console her for the berating she was certainly going to receive.

While the tea was being ordered, Ellen had a moment to look about. The room into which she had been ushered was enormous. It was paneled in dark old wood, and furnished with elaborate period pieces. The wood of the furniture had been polished to a mirror-like sheen, but it was crumbling with age. Ellen had an impression of generations of moths rearing their young through childhood, love, and successful parenthood in the threadbare folds of the gold damask draperies at the windows.

While they waited for the tea, Aunt Minna unlocked a cupboard to remove a silver biscuit box. She was not in fact so tall as she had seemed at Ellen's first glance, not much taller than her niece. The hat, with its feathers, and her bearing, gave her an extra foot or so. She stopped fussing with the tea table to observe her guest. She might have been looking over some piece of furniture that she was thinking of buying. Her only comment when she had concluded the inspection was, 'You have good bones.'

The fresh tea arrived. Aunt Minna poured it with graceful ease, and offered some surprisingly fresh chocolate cookies from the silver box.

'Now,' she said, 'tell me about your mother. She seemed most anxious to have you away somewhere. I don't suppose she is conducting a romance?' She smiled to show Ellen this was meant to be preposterous, and Ellen smiled in return.

'I think she was frightened to have me in the house.'

'You don't look particularly frightening. You were in an insane asylum?'

'I was in a private hospital.'

'For the insane.'

'For the mentally disturbed.'

Aunt Mina looked at her sharply. She wondered if her niece were trying to quarrel with her. She decided it was quite possible.

'Is that what you were, mentally disturbed?'

'No, I was insane.' Ellen smiled to show this was meant to be preposterous.

Aunt Minna gave a deep appreciative chuckle and took a bite out of a chocolate cookie. 'How do you know you're sane now?'

Ellen shrugged. She was enjoying herself. She liked this peculiar old woman who, from some chance of birth, was her aunt. 'How do you know you are?'

'You've got a point there. A great many people would say I'm not. You may say that yourself when you have been here a time.' She reached for the tea to pour some more.

Ellen said, 'Tell me about the moon garden.'

'So you remember that, do you?'

'Only that there was something called that. Mother said it was haunted, but she declined to tell me much more than that.'

'She would. Your mother has always been timid.' She made of that word a scornful dismissal. Ellen could not imagine anything more removed from Aunt Minna's own character than timidity.

There was a noise from the door. Ellen's back was to it, so that she could not see who had come into the room. Whoever it was had apparently paused just inside. Perhaps they were surprised by her presence.

Since they did not come forward, and she could hardly turn on her seat to see who it was, she went on with her conversation as if they were not there.

'How did it get such an odd name? The moon garden. Surely it's pre-astronaut, isn't it?'

A man's voice said, 'No one uses the moon garden now, it's been shut up for ages.'

Aunt Minna rose, saying, 'Come in, Dawson, come in, I want you to meet my niece, Ellen Miles. Ellen, this is Dawson Elliott.'

Ellen remained where she was, a pink and gilt china cup in her hand. Dawson Elliot came about the settee to greet her. He was good-looking, in a faded sort of way, and not so sure of himself, she thought, as he would like to appear. Although it was an old-fashioned word, 'mountebank' came to mind. He was a little more pleased to make her acquaintance then ought to be possible at such short notice. His face crinkled into those pre-arranged lines of charm that good-looking people assume so easily.

'Mr. Elliott is a writer,' Aunt Minna said. 'He's doing a book on old homes of the south, and naturally he wanted to include this one.'

'It's quite a treasure,' he said. 'We weren't expecting you until tomorrow.'

'She said in her letter she was coming on the nineteenth,' Aunt Minna said. 'Look, it's right here.'

She went to one of the rosewood writing tables and rummaging through some papers on its surface, picked up a sheet of paper. From where she sat, Ellen could see at once that it was her letter, but Aunt Minna's eyes scanned it quickly, and she put it aside.

'Now I can't find the letter,' she said, turning away from the desk. 'Dawson, ring for Bondage and tell her you want some tea.'

'No need for her to run up and down

the steps,' he said. 'I'll slip down and tell her. Excuse me, ladies.'

'Mr. Eliot is staying in the house,' Aunt Minna said when he was gone, as if she thought some explanation were needed.

'I see,' Ellen said. She did not know what to think of that. She thought finally it was probably none of her business, and she had better refrain from commenting upon it.

Dawson Elliott was back in a moment, followed by Mrs. Bondage with a second teapot. Dawson himself carried a China plate of petit-fours which he started to set on the table before Ellen. Aunt Minna countered with a magniloquent, 'These are the best,' and whipping the lid off her silver box, planted it down before Ellen with such sudden recklessness that Dawson had to snatch his own offering to safety.

They had more tea, although Ellen was feeling saturated by now. Finally, Aunt Minna rose and put out her hand toward her niece. 'Come along, my dear, and see your room. Did you bring your luggage?'

'It's at the airport.'

'Never mind, Pomfret can get it later.'

'I feel like I'm imposing. If I had known you already had company . . . '

'Nonsense.' Minna threw open the door. 'I shall like having you. And Dawson isn't company, he's only a writer.' There was the faintest twinkle in her eye as she said this, as though she were up to some devilment, the nature of which eluded Ellen.

They went up a wide stairway to the third floor. The room that was to be Ellen's had a canopied four-poster, garlanded ivory walls, and a lovely view from the window of the river and some green trees, spread out like a tapestry.

The room was not quite ready, however, with the bedclothes in a stack on the bare mattress. Minna was furious. 'Ring for Mrs. Bondage,' she said, indicating the bell pull, 'and tell her to get this in order at once. We were expecting you tomorrow of course, but still . . . '

'There's no need to make a fuss over me,' Ellen said. 'I can make the bed by myself. It's easier, actually.'

'Oh well, easier,' Aunt Minna said disdainfully. 'It's easier to lie down then to stand up. The easiest thing of all is to be a vegetable, so far as that goes.'

Ellen rang the bell as she had asked. Aunt Minna had gone to the window, and Ellen followed.

'It's lovely,' she said.

'Yes. That's the Savannah River. Down there, though you can't see it from here for the trees, we have our own little inlet and dock, so we have ocean access still, by the river. Not many houses can boast that. And from the other side, from the window in the hall, you can see the whole terrace. It used to be so much nicer I'm afraid.'

Ellen leaned forward a little, out the window. Off to the left, through the trees, she could see a yellow house, a cottage. As she looked in that direction, she thought a curtain moved, as if it had been held aside and then, as she looked, allowed to fall.

'Who lives there?'

Aunt Minna followed her glance. 'Oh, there. It's the Creighton's guest cottage, but they've let it. That's what has happened to the terrace, people letting houses to any riffraff that comes along.'

'They have rented to somebody unsavory, have they?' Ellen was amused at her aunt's rigid social sense.

'That's exactly what they've done. The man's a writer.'

'Isn't Dawson Elliott a writer?'

'Yes. But this man writes romances. I have no doubt what kind of romances, either. And he's a northerner. His name is, let me see, Parker. Yes, Mr. Kenneth Parker. I looked in the *Who's Who*, but there are no writers listed by that name. You won't want to mix with him, dear. Ah, here's Bondage.'

★   ★   ★

Dawson Elliott smoked a cigarette, pacing the length of the sitting room and then, since Minna had not yet returned, smoked a second cigarette. A window was open upon the street, and he went to it. On the table by it was the old telescope she used to spy on people.

29

Minna entered from the hall, sniffing the air disapprovingly. He did not put out his cigarette, but he did stay by the window so that the gentle breeze carried the smoke away.

'Well?' he asked.

'Bondage is making the bed for her,' she said, which had nothing to do with what was worrying him. 'She'll be comfortable there, I'm certain.'

'What brought her a day early?' he asked, determined not to be put off. 'You don't suppose . . . ?'

Minna's dark eyes flashed. She knew perfectly well what was bothering him. 'Don't be ignorant,' she snapped. 'We must make little allowances. She got her dates mixed up. I myself would have been more accurate, but she's been ill. Who left the lid off that box?' She snatched up the lid for the silver cookie box and clapped it into place.

'It's most inconvenient.' He tossed his cigarette outside. 'Having her here tonight.'

She stood for a moment in thoughtful silence, staring at the silver box but seeing, he was sure, something quite different.

'She's very tired,' she said on a note of finality. 'I expect she'll sleep very soundly tonight.'

I hope so, he thought, but he did not voice the thought aloud. He wondered if there was an innuendo in her statement, something to be read between the lines. Did she mean to ensure that the girl slept very soundly? There was no telling, and no use asking.

Asking, in fact, might be very bad. He had made one grave mistake already, when he had strongly opposed having that girl here at all. He knew, without ever being told, that his resistance to the idea had helped her decide to have her niece come. If she once thought you were trying to make her do something, she was determined at any cost to do the opposite. And the girl was put in the role of an underdog. The old woman so loved a loser.

'If you'll excuse me,' he said, 'I'll go to my own room.'

'Dawson,' she said as he was going out

the door, 'I don't think Ellen will interfere.'

When she said it, she could not see what Dawson saw: Ellen approaching down the hall, close enough to hear that remark.

'Interfere with what?' she asked, from the door.

Dawson looked perturbed, but Minna, without batting a lash, said, 'Why, with Dawson's book, darling.'

Dawson fled.

3

Ellen woke with a start. For just a moment, she did not know where she was. She thought she was still at Lawndale, in that cold, institutional room with its wire-mesh-covered windows. She lay with her eyes closed, trying to recall the dream that had wakened her, listening without any real attention to the murmur of voices in the hall outside. One of the patients must be causing trouble, she thought.

Then she remembered — this was not Lawndale, but Aunt Minna's home in Savannah. And the voices, she realized, opening her eyes, were not coming from the hall, but from outside.

She slipped out of bed and went to the window, but the voices had stopped. She listened and heard a whispering sound, but she could not say for certain whether it was really people whispering, or only the wind in the trees. Perhaps she had not heard voices at all. Perhaps it had only been a remnant of her dream.

Something flickered through the trees, gleamed briefly, and was gone. It might have been someone walking with a flashlight. Or it might have been a boat on the river.

Or I might have imagined it, she told herself. She felt restless. She turned and crossed the dark room, to the door.

She was not imagining that the door was locked. She tried it timidly, and then with some force. It was plainly locked.

She stepped back from it, staring at the faint gleam of the brass knob. Even in Lawndale she had not been locked into her room. She had not been considered violent, only . . .

But what did Aunt Minna know of these distinctions? Aunt Minna had obviously considered her dangerous, dangerous enough that she must be locked up like a caged animal at night.

She had gone to bed earlier with a sense of happiness and a feeling of confidence. When she returned to her bed now it was to huddle like a frightened chick, pulling the covers close up under her chin and staring for long time at the molding about the ceiling.

★ ★ ★

'You must be mistaken, dear. You can see for yourself the door isn't locked.' Aunt Minna moved the door pointedly to and fro.

'It was locked,' Ellen insisted; but she added, less firmly, 'I thought it was.' More than that, she had known that it was. But it had not been locked in the morning, and Aunt Minna knew nothing about it, and Ellen was sure those dark eyes were not concealing a lie.

So unless she accepted the idea that one of the servants, or Dawson Elliott, had stolen along the hall in the night to lock her in, and again later to unlock the door, the only conclusion was that she must somehow have been mistaken. And considering what the past year had been like for her, that was not a very pleasant idea to contemplate.

'What has happened,' Minna said,

apparently dismissing the matter as of no consequence, 'is that you've had a bad dream and you're having a little difficulty this morning remembering that it was a dream. I assure you, my child, locking people in their rooms is not my style. And even if it were, what possible reason do you think I could have?'

She looked at her niece and because Ellen looked so miserable, she suddenly understood.

'I assure you,' Minna said with a tenderness quite uncommon to her, 'I had put that matter completely out of my thoughts. And now I think it's time you did the same. Come, dry those tears, and let's put things in order here, shall we?'

It was Saturday. Aunt Minna had decided Ellen's room must be rearranged, and she personally must supervise it. Ellen, relieved to know that she hadn't been locked in like a dangerous animal (although it was a bit frightening to think she was having trouble separating reality from dreams) stood by and watched in awe.

Minna seemed set on dispelling any

gloom by the practice of much busyness. Every few minutes she would think of something more that was needed to make the room comfortable.

She had Mrs. Bondage, and Bertha, and a frail looking elderly gentleman who turned out to be Pomfret, flying up and down the stairs in a whirlwind of activity.

In the process, Ellen learned that these three made up the servant staff, and that the two women came days, while Pomfret lived in a room in the basement. She learned a good deal too of Minna's attitudes regarding servants.

'You must see that they take care of things,' Aunt Minna warned her. 'See that they do what you ask them. Servants get some strange ideas these days. Pomfret talked to me once about days off. Can you imagine? Days off! And you must see that they have things to do for you, even if it's unnecessary. Otherwise they don't respect you, and then they become impossible.'

She would interrupt these monologues at frequent intervals to flay the servants with her tongue. These scoldings seemed to disturb Ellen more than the staff, and after a time she began to realize that the servants were quite accustomed and attached little if any importance to them.

Ellen must have a tea caddy and a silver service, in case she wanted tea in her room. The dressing table was placed wrong for the light, and it must be moved. The new position was equally bad, but satisfied the older woman. There must be a writing table, and paper, and an inkstand.

It was clear that Aunt Minna was enjoying herself, but for Ellen it was a welcome change, all this purposeful bustle, and no one giving a hoot if her feelings were hurt over something, or watching what they said to be sure they did not offend. Aunt Minna had no hesitation in calling someone crazy. She apparently considered all but a handful of Savannah's residents to be in that condition.

She was also, Ellen decided, the most tireless stander ever known. When Ellen suggested she supervise the work from a chair, Minna waved the suggestion away.

So they both stood, because Ellen did not want to admit to greater weakness, and if her aunt thought of her niece's comfort in this respect, she did not once mention it.

At last Minna seemed to think the room satisfactory, and retired to her own sitting room. Ellen herself was exhausted by such tireless energy. She sat at the writing table, remembering that she must write a note to her mother to tell her she had arrived and was safely installed in the house. She found at once that the ink in the massive silver and glass inkstand had long since dried to dust. She got a ballpoint pen from her purse and wrote her note.

She made it succinct. She could not, without alarming her mother, say, 'You were right, Aunt Minna is as crazy as a loon, and I love her.'

No good telling her mother about the mix-up in dates, either; that would only worry her. She knew the house, so it needn't be described, and she would not take well to the idea that it was crumbling into dust. And if she knew that Aunt

Minna had another house guest, a single man who was young and good looking, and a writer, well . . .

What she told her mother was that she had arrived safely, she found house and aunt both charming, and was feeling very much at peace already. That, she felt confident, was what her mother would need to hear.

She addressed the envelope and, sealing it, took it downstairs with her. Her aunt was not about, but Bondage was scurrying along the hall on one of her errands, and Ellen asked her what to do about mailing the letter.

'Just leave it with me, miss,' Bondage said. 'I'll see Pomfret takes it down to the station with the other mail.'

'Does he go regularly?' Ellen asked, thinking she ought to know if there was a schedule, so that she could suit her letter writing to it.

'Yes, ma'am. Mr. Elliott does a lot of mailing, to do with his book, I suppose. Pomfret goes just after lunch every day.'

'I'll remember, and thank you,' Ellen said, handing the letter over.

'You're welcome, I'm sure.' Bondage bobbed her head and, smiling cheerfully, went on her way.

It was not yet lunchtime. Ellen felt very much on her own. She wandered through a few of the downstairs rooms. They spoke of a life that was much more elegant than today's. She saw these rooms filled with ladies in crinoline. An army of servants would post and speed. Outside, the terrace would be lined solid with fine carriages.

She laughed at her reveries. Someone, she forgot who, had said that one's reverence for the past was just in proportion to one's ignorance of it.

And what of her aunt? She lived in the past, although she could hardly be said to be ignorant of it.

She had come to the end of the hall. A door opened onto a small back terrace, overhung with bougainvillea. From the terrace she could see a path running into the trees. This, she decided, glancing around to get her bearings, would be the path down to the river.

It was shady, and when the summer

heat was really up it would be a delight to escape it here. Fallen leaves from other seasons made a soft, thick carpet underneath, and the air had a damp, earthy smell that was soothing. She thought it must have been from here that she had heard those voices and seen the light during the night.

If, she thought, frowning, there had been any voices, or any light. Or had the two been a part of her strange dream?

The path twisted through the trees, breaking for a moment at a clearing lush with honeysuckle. Here the way divided, one fork running uphill, the other continuing down.

The one that went up, she thought looking in that direction, must go up to the yellow cottage she had seen through the trees. She continued on the path down to the river, past a magnolia tree in riotous bloom.

The carpeting of leaves made her steps silent. She came in sight of the water: a little inlet, a miniature cove that branched off the river. A crude little dock, the wood old and gray, had been built into the water from the muddy bank.

The water too was gray, and deep green, and dappled with yellow where the sunlight broke through the trees. The perfumes of honeysuckle and magnolia, and the ripe earth, blended with a sweet-sour river scent, assaulting the nostrils. The stillness was broken by the trilling of a bird somewhere in the trees, and a gentle lapping of water against the wooden pilings.

She was not alone after all. There was a man on the dock, his back to her: a young man, slim, with muscles rippling over his back where his shirt was stretched taut. He knelt at the end of the wooden planking, bending far forward to look at something.

He did not hear her, of course, because her approach was so noiseless, and he was so absorbed in whatever it was he was examining. And because he was so quiet, she herself could not think to make any noise, or announce her presence.

She stepped onto the rotted wood of the dock, and then he heard her, or perhaps, felt her presence. His reaction was sudden and startling. He seemed in one violent movement to stand and turn, like a skater making a stupendous leap.

He was suddenly facing her, crouched slightly as if ready to spring, and his hands at his side were half clenched.

She was nearly as surprised as he. She looked at that long, oval face with the pale blue eyes that seemed to blaze with a light from within, and recognized him at once.

She had seen him only a few days before, in Cincinnati. Then, he had been following her across the fountain square, watching her so closely that he had collided with another woman.

It was strange to meet him again, like this. She did not know which was the most awkward, that sudden attitude of hostility, or the air of embarrassment that followed it.

She felt quite foolish, as if she had done something wrong but did not exactly know what it was. She could think of nothing to say. She gazed into those blue, blue eyes, the most striking she had ever seen.

He relaxed, and grinned too brightly. 'Hello,' he said. 'You must be Miss Miles' niece.'

She nodded. She wished she could think of something clever to say. She had always admired women who could do that with ease.

He, however, seemed to have no difficulty. 'I'm Ken Parker,' he said. 'A neighbor, sort of. I rent the Creightons' guest house up the hill there.'

'We've met before,' she said, 'in a manner of speaking.'

He lifted an eyebrow. 'Have we? I don't recall.' With a smile, he added, 'And I'm sure I would remember you.'

'It was only a few days ago. We didn't really meet, we just saw one another across the square. In Cincinnati.'

He looked puzzled. 'I don't think so.'

She felt embarrassed. She saw how he or anyone else would see it. He had not even noticed her, just another girl crossing a square, who happened ever so fleetingly to catch his eye. While she, poor foolish creature, acted as if the scene were emblazoned on her heart.

'It was very brief,' she stammered, feeling increasingly foolish with each word. 'You ran into a woman with her arms filled with packages. Perhaps you didn't even see me, but I saw you.'

He shook his head. 'Cincinnati, you say? Then you must be mistaken. I've never been to that city, that I recall. Certainly not in the past few days.'

He smiled apologetically. She looked mortified. 'But it was . . . ' she began, and stopped herself.

She knew how wrong her own impressions could be. She hadn't the confidence in her memory or judgment to defend it in an argument. She had recently spent a year at a mental hospital because her thought processes couldn't be trusted. And the trouble wasn't all that far away, either. There was last night too, the door she had thought was locked, hearing voices . . . She was mortified to have exposed herself as such a fool before a perfect stranger.

'I'm sorry.' She looked down at her shoes. 'I must have been mistaken.'

'No, it is I who am sorry. I would like

to have seen you before. I wish this were only one of many meetings, and that we were already well enough acquainted that you wouldn't look as if you would jump into the river if I tried to touch you.'

She tried not to be flattered too much by that remark, and then not to laugh as she envisioned what he had described; but despite herself, the corners of her mouth turned up.

'That's better.' He put his hand on her arm, and she did in fact start a little, but she did not jump into the water. 'Come on, I'll walk you partway back to the house.'

She let him direct her up the path, down which she had just come, not because she was in such a hurry to get back to the house, but because she was too embarrassed to protest.

'What were you looking for?' she asked, trying to fill the empty space between them. 'At the landing.'

He chuckled. 'Your imagination must be working overtime.'

She stiffened. It was beginning to look as if nothing that she observed was real.

'You were,' she said sharply, very sharply.

'Hey, are you angry?' He stopped to look down at her. Now she was embarrassed at her sharp tongue, and looked away from him. 'Look,' he said, 'I was trespassing and I apologize for that. It's such a pretty spot, very peaceful. When you came up I was watching some sort of water bug having a swim. I suppose it must have looked to you like I was hunting for something. End of quarrel?'

'I didn't mean to quarrel. I am sorry.'

'Now don't go looking tortured, either' he said. 'Everybody isn't waiting to slap you into a dungeon, you know.'

She laughed, because he was pleasant, and she forgot about the landing and the way he had seemed to be looking for something.

'It is Ellen, isn't it?' he asked as they climbed. He was careful to push any threatening branches out of her way.

She looked up at him. 'Yes. How did you know?'

'Oh, we've all been hearing about you, and that you were coming for a visit.'

Her face reddened, and she looked straight ahead again. And, she thought, in an agony of mortification, you've heard why my visit was necessary, and how I've spent my last year. She thought of yesterday, when she had looked from her window and seen the yellow cottage. She had thought then someone was watching. Had he said to someone within, 'That must be her, the crazy niece'?

'Careful,' he said, holding her arm firmly and putting his free arm about her. She had stumbled on the tree root. 'Hey, you're shaking.'

'I'm not,' she said quickly, and realized that sounded really silly, since anyone with a right mind could see she was shaking like a leaf.

But how could she have explained that, apart from her father, no man had ever put his arm about her, even to keep her from falling? That she had never had an opportunity to learn to flirt, as he seemed to be flirting with her?

As it turned out there was no need to explain, because they had come into the clearing where the paths separated; and there, coming down the path from Minna's house, was Dawson Elliott.

He looked relieved to see her — too relieved, she thought — and then at once she told herself, Oh, God, you're seeing something nasty in everything, and that isn't good.

He was less happy to see Ken Parker. The two men eyed each other in a manner that was considerably less friendly. Ellen saw, too, that Dawson noticed Ken's arm, still about her waist. Ken did not hasten to remove it, and she could not help feeling a little pleased at that.

There was an awkward silence. Dawson said, 'Hello, I was just coming to see if you were down this way.'

'Why?' she asked.

He blushed, and she saw at once that she was not being too suspicious. That he had been worrying about her, that he thought she was not safe on her own. He was watching over her, and she didn't like it. She had done with that when she left Lawndale.

'It's nearly lunchtime,' he said, but not

soon enough to save the moment. 'Hello, Parker.'

Ken nodded. 'Dawson.'

'Then you know one another,' Ellen said.

'Oh yes,' Dawson said, sounding not very enthusiastic. 'We know one another. Fellow writers, so it would seem.'

Ken released her finally. 'I don't want to hold you up from lunch. I've enjoyed showing you the river, Miss Miles. I trust I'll have the pleasure again.'

His eyes sparkled. She said, 'Since we live so close, it's almost inevitable, isn't it?'

'I hope so.' She thought he looked genuinely pleased at the prospect. He bent to kiss the back of her hand.

'What was he doing at the river?' Dawson asked when he had gone.

She shrugged. 'I have no idea.' She went past him and started back for the house. She felt vaguely annoyed with Dawson for watching over her as she was sure he was doing. Keeping an eye on her, was probably the way he and her aunt put it.

In any event, she was disinclined to discuss Ken Parker with him. Mr. Parker was very much in her thoughts, but they were thoughts she preferred to keep to herself.

He was certainly the most exciting man she had ever met. Not, in fact, that she had met so very many men. Her parents between them, her father especially, had kept her insulated from life. And when she'd tried to break away, there had been the fire. She knew, logically, that the fire had been an accident, a drunken man's accident, but that hadn't stopped the guilt from nearly destroying her. So, she knew very little about men being interested in her. But she had gotten the impression that Ken Parker was.

And that very exciting idea she did not care to discuss with Dawson.

4

At luncheon, she said, 'I still haven't heard about the moon garden. Or seen it, for that matter. Does it exist, or is the whole thing merely a figment of someone's imagination?'

'It exists,' Dawson said. 'It's one of my reasons for choosing this house as, shall we say, a home base.'

'It's kept locked,' Minna said.

Ellen saw a glance that her aunt did not care for this line of conversation. She wondered if Aunt Minna might have resented Dawson's choice of words. The older woman would not like to think that someone had 'chosen' her house to stay in, and simply moved in. Undoubtedly it had been managed in such a way that she had extended an invitation.

'But it can be unlocked,' Dawson said. 'Your aunt thinks it's a gloomy place, but she doesn't see it with the historian's eye.'

Despite the fact that Aunt Minna

continued to look sulky, Dawson seemed intent on explaining the moon garden to Ellen. A sense of loyalty on Ellen's part made her think briefly that perhaps she ought to discourage the conversation, but Dawson had begun to talk, a pastime that apparently gave him a great deal of pleasure, and she listened with interest.

'In the past,' he explained, sipping the pale white wine Mrs. Bondage had served with the cold chicken, 'the house was used for slave running. It was built with that in mind, and a garden was attached, windowless and high-walled. It wasn't a real garden, mind you, just an open space connected with the basement room in which the slaves were kept. It was the slaves who gave it the name, moon garden. They were only allowed out in it at night, so there was no risk of their disturbing the ladies of the house. Perhaps they gave it that name because the moon was the only adornment the space had in those days, I don't know — its only flower, if you will permit a bit of poetry.'

Dawson talked well, with a nice

inflection, and the flair of the natural born storyteller, so the scene seemed to come to life before Ellen's eyes, as she gazed into her wine glass. She saw the dark garden, nothing more than hard-packed earth surrounded by the wood and brick of its walls. It was night and the moon gave a silvery luster to the scene.

Then, from some underground room, came the dark figures of the slaves — men and women, even children, shuffling forlornly out. They would be frightened, heartbroken, despairing. How long since they had been ripped from their homes, herded into ships like cattle, carried across a terrifying ocean to a new and not so brave world? Those basements in which they cowered must have been as the pits of hell to them. And then, for a moment, respite. A few minutes of freedom. To climb upward and suddenly see the one thing left that was familiar and serene, the silvery moon above.

A bit of poetry? It must have made their hearts ache with its unchained loveliness, so distant, so calm. The garden of the moon. Yes, she could understand how they had named it that.

'For a time,' Dawson went on, 'the slave running was a highly profitable trade. A fortune was made farming that little garden. Nothing grew there but the souls of men, and those fragile blooms withered and died.

'Then, sometime before the Civil War, an event happened. Some called it a tragedy. I'm not so sure it was. It may have been a blessing, in a sense. For those poor people. The ships had just come in. The place was crowded with slaves, jammed into the basement with scarcely space to turn around, let alone to lie down to sleep. And even so there wasn't room for all. The blacks who couldn't crowd into the basement were left in the garden. The master of the house was already counting the rich profit he would make. A railroad line was soon to be laid clear across the deep South and he had a contract to supply all the labor. He had invested everything. For a day it had seemed as if his fortune might be lost. A storm had chased the ships across the sea.

'But they had outrun it, reached the

safety of the harbor, and finally the little cove here. Now the slaves were in the basement and crowded into the moon garden, and he could drink a glass of port in this very room and say thanks to whatever powers had seen him in safely.

'The storm was a hurricane, unfortunately. He had outrun it, but he hadn't lost it. It struck old Savannah like an atomic bomb attack. Flattened houses, drowned horses, pulled trees right out of the ground.

'The family was all right. This house is as solid as Gibraltar, and when the storm started really blowing, they boarded themselves up in here. But he had brought in almost two hundred slaves and more than a hundred of them were out there in the garden, nothing but the filthy rags they wore to protect them from the worst storm ever to hit the seaboard.'

Ellen's eyes were wide with horror. She could see the terrified slaves, shaking with the cold and the rain, crying perhaps to gods of their own, gods of the distant jungle, for mercy. What a scene of terror there must have been! She heard the scream of the driving winds and above that, the screams of those frightened creatures. A shudder swept through her.

'Couldn't they have brought them inside?' she asked.

Dawson smiled. 'This was the Old South, and these were slaves. Not even trained slaves yet, but savages, fresh from the jungles.'

He paused for a sip of his wine. The room was charged with the drama of that old tale. Even Minna sat in thoughtful silence, as if she too were reliving that dreadful scene.

'Scores died,' Dawson said. 'And in the end, the man who had left them out in that storm paid for his cruelty. He was ruined. He could not sustain the losses, not only all his cash, but he had mortgaged the house as well, and his ships, to raise the money for this venture. He sold the slaves he had left, but the money was not enough. He lost the ships, and since they were his source of income, he lost the rest soon afterward.

'The history of the house did a striking turnabout then. The War was not far off.

Anti-slavery sentiment was already running high and the man who next came into possession of the house sympathized with the North.'

Aunt Minna sniffed loudly, but said nothing.

'The story got about that the house was haunted. Scarcely anyone wanted to come near it. Schoolboys who crept close at night on dares said they could hear the whispering of the dead slaves from the hidden garden, and sometimes they saw the slaves making their way along the path that led from the house to the landing.'

Ellen saw suddenly where he was leading. 'The underground railroad,' she exclaimed.

He beamed at her. 'Right you are. The house was perfect for it, with the landing giving access to the ocean and the hidden garden. For a time it was the most important escape point in the South for runaway slaves.

'But in time tragedy struck again. Eventually local people came to suspect the source of the ghost stories and the meaning of the whispering and the figures stealing along the path at night.

'One night a band of white vigilantes stormed the house. The master of the house was away, transporting a band of runaways. The wife was alone with her servants and a handful of runaway slaves. She was a brave woman, and tried to prevent their entering the house. In the ensuing fracas, she and several of the slaves were killed.'

Dawson sat for a moment in silence. The candles on the table flickered in a draft. 'After this second tragedy, the house was truly looked upon as haunted. It passed into the hands of a cousin, who was of course an ancestor of your aunt's, and thus to a new branch of the family. The moon garden was closed up. For a while someone planted it with flowers, but in time it was abandoned.'

'It has been unused since,' Aunt Minna said. 'I think we've had enough of this gloomy talk. Let's go into the library.'

'Oh, I don't think it's gloomy,' Ellen said. 'It's all very romantic. Can I see the garden?'

'I'll show it to you now, if you like,' Dawson said, smiling. 'That is, if your aunt doesn't mind.'

'Why should I mind?' Aunt Minna said. 'Though why you should want to see a few scraggly old bushes and some spiders, I can't think.'

Her reply was so sharp that Ellen had a strange impression that she did in fact mind but did not want to say so.

'I suppose it isn't really necessary,' Ellen said a trifle reluctantly.

'Nonsense,' Dawson said, 'Don't let your aunt scare you off. She talks of the entire place most disparagingly, because it's all familiar to her. I find the house utterly fascinating, including the garden. Come with me.'

They went into the library. Its walls were paneled with old, dark wood, and two of the walls were lined with shelves of books from floor to ceiling.

Dawson put his hand behind a row of books, feeling about. Ellen heard a click. To her amazement, Dawson took a firm hold of the shelf, and swung aside an entire section of wall, its shelves and books intact, to reveal a door leading outside.

'It's scary, Ellen said, stepping through the opening. 'Like something out of the movies.'

She was in the moon garden. There was even a moon. The mist had come up from the river, drifting gently on the evening breeze.

The garden was surprisingly small, fifteen or twenty feet square, though it was perhaps generous to call it a garden. There was only the earth, packed solid, and a few tufts of dried grass. That, and some bushes that had once been roses and a stone seat, covered with moss.

Its name seemed oddly appropriate. Despite the few plants, the garden was as inhospitable looking as one of those views of the moon's surface taken by the astronauts.

On the ground, at the far end of a garden, wooden doors lay nearly flat upon the ground.

'They lead to the slave cells,' Dawson said. 'It's a sort of a second basement, quite unconnected with the one in which

Pomfret sleeps. Would you like to see it?'

'She most certainly would not,' Minna declared firmly. 'It's utterly filthy, and quite unsafe. What a thing to even suggest!'

Ellen was startled by her aunt's vehemence, and when she looked at Dawson she saw a mischievous glint in his eye. He was only joking. Apparently he knew that the cellars were unsafe, and was teasing Minna.

'I'm not very fond of cellars anyway,' Ellen said. 'How did they get them in and out of here, except through the house?'

'There's a door over here. It's hidden, of course; you have to know where to look. Here, you see?'

He touched a section of wall and a door clicked open onto the woods behind the house.

'Of course it was kept locked in the past. This is the catch for the outside.'

'It's cold out here.' Minna shivered. 'Let's go back in.'

Ellen thought it rather pleasantly warm, but she went with them back toward the house. Glancing up, she saw a single window overlooking the garden.

'I don't place that window in the house,' she said.

'That's because from the inside it's hidden too,' Dawson explained. 'It's high so that the master could look down into the garden, but there's no risk of a slave breaking into the house proper. It opens into the upstairs hall, but there's a highboy in front of it that conceals it.'

'I remember it,' Ellen said. 'Yes, I can almost feel the presence of tragedy here. Oh look, what's this?'

She bent to pick up a piece of crumpled paper from behind the one wild-growing rose. It was an empty cigarette pack. She laughed and held it up for Dawson to see.

'Well, unless ghosts have started smoking, someone has been here lately.'

'I probably threw it away myself,' Dawson said. 'I must admit it was sloppy of me, wasn't it?'

'It isn't your brand.'

He took it and examined it, and crumpling it into a ball, dropping it into his pocket. 'I change brands occasionally.

Or, more than likely, someone going by outside tossed it over the wall. I shouldn't worry about it if I were you.'

'No one uses this garden,' Minna said.

Dawson had taken Ellen's arm again and she was steered gently but firmly back into the house. As the hidden door swung closed, sealing off the moon garden, Ellen had another glimpse of the high wall that concealed the moon garden from the world outside.

It seemed to her unlikely that anyone would be just passing by on the private path outside. But even more unlikely was the prospect that they should have tried to toss a cigarette pack over a three-story wall. She had the most peculiar feeling that Dawson and her aunt were trying to conceal something from her.

And that, my girl, she told herself, turning her back on the hidden door, is the road that leads to paranoia . . . and back to Lawndale.

She dismissed the thought from her mind completely.

★   ★   ★

Ken Parker moved through the mist in a nonchalant way, but his footsteps were silent, and his dark trousers and jacket gave him a ghostlike quality. He seemed to emerge suddenly from the mist, drift silently by, and disappear again.

He was at the city's waterfront. A shape loomed up in the distance, grew, and became a sailing ship at rest in the river. It was a three-masted square rigger, a museum piece now, but it was like those ships that once crossed the wild Atlantic bearing cargoes of cotton and indigo. In the night, in the mist, the sight of that old ship gave an eerie sensation, as if one had stepped across the frontiers of time, and into the world of the past.

In the distance behind him a car sounded its horn and he was jolted back to the present. He went another step or two, and saw the modern day riverboats close at hand, and the illusion died.

In another moment he heard footsteps, very soft, and was alert at once. He looked relaxed, unwary; but in fact he was tensed, ready to spring if need be.

A man emerged from the mist. Parker

saw the way the man walked and recognized the set of the shoulders. Nielsen.

'Let's walk,' Nielsen said. They fell into step together, strolling idly as if they had nothing in particular on their minds.

'Well?' Nielsen said after a moment.

'It's the same girl. I don't think she's in on anything, though.'

'What makes you think that?'

'Intuition.'

'Not good enough. You've got to find out what she does know. And even if she doesn't know anything, she's your entrée into the house. Sleep with her if you've got to.'

'I don't think that'll be necessary,' Parker said quickly.

A little too quickly, Nielsen thought. He glanced briefly in Parker's direction. Something about the set of his chin bothered him. He looked sore, although he was too much in control of himself to really display that sort of emotion. But something . . .

Now what the hell? Nielsen thought, annoyed. Something had put his back up, and all of a sudden. This girl? That wasn't possible. He knew too much about Parker's lifestyle. Parker wasn't the sort to get excited about a pretty girl. Sex from time to time, yes, but strictly on the functional level. And even if he were susceptible to an emotional entanglement, there hadn't been time for anything like that.

'Have you talked to her much?' he asked, feeling for some clue.

'Briefly. Once.'

'What, you've already decided she's not involved?' Nielsen emphasized the incredulity of it.

'I'll look into it further.' Again, his tone was just a little too crisp.

Nielsen didn't like it. He had a nose for trouble, which was what had made him so successful in his field. And he smelled something here that was, if not rotten, just not right. If Parker had gotten emotionally involved — but he couldn't have, after one meeting. Still, it could be a good idea to keep a finger to the pulse.

'Do that,' he said aloud.

They walked a bit further, talking in

low voices, and then retraced their steps to the old sailing ship, where they parted. There were no handshakes, no words of a farewell.

Nielsen drifted away as inconspicuously as he had appeared and a short time later, Parker walked back to his own car, and went home.

5

Why, Ellen wondered, should Dawson steal so furtively from the house at such a late hour? It was nearly 2 a.m. She had been dreaming and had wakened with a start. At once she thought of that other night's dream and slipped from her bed. Her door was unlocked, so this was not the same dream.

She went to the window. At first she saw nothing. Then as she stared, she saw a tree that was different from the others. She realized it was not a tree at all, but the sail of a boat. She studied its location, and thought it must be at the landing below.

Minna had told her the landing was unused. Certainly it was a private landing for the house, so no one else had any right using it.

Should she tell her aunt? It could be something quite harmless, and her aunt might not appreciate being awakened at this hour.

While she debated with herself she heard a sound from the hall. She went cautiously to the door again, listening.

Yes, certainly those were footsteps, stealthy but unmistakable on the creaking floor of the old house. She paused and waited. The sounds stopped outside her door. Someone was standing beyond it, listening, just as she was listening. If they opened the door, they would be face-to-face with her.

The footsteps went away. She waited, trembling, unsure, but she had to know. She opened the door as carefully as she could.

She had a glimpse of Dawson, dressed all in dark clothes, disappearing down the stairs. She waited until he was well out of sight. Then she went into the hall and listened. She heard a door close below.

She went back into her room, hurrying to the window. It was still there, that triangle of white. It had not vanished, as she had feared it might.

Why would Dawson be stealing out of the house like that in the middle of the night? The question buzzed like a troublesome fly through her mind. Was it something to do with the boat at the landing? Was there some sort of trouble, with which she might be able to help?

* * *

Dawson stood deep in the shadows thrown by the trees. Except for the glow of his cigarette, one could have passed within inches of him and not known that he was there.

Hearing a sound in the trees, he put his cigarette on the ground and carefully crushed it out with his foot.

Someone appeared. Dawson stepped out from the shadows and spoke in a low voice. The man replied, and Dawson relaxed slightly.

'This way,' he said. The man followed him to the door into the moon garden.

* * *

It was not only curiosity that impelled Ellen to leave her room and move on stealthy feet down the stairs. She wanted to know, with certainty, that these strange things were not more figments of her imagination. She could not bear to think that dreams were becoming real for her. She knew where that must inevitably lead.

Downstairs, though, there was no clue to tell her where Dawson had gone, or why. She came into the library, and paused as a flicker of movement beyond the French doors caught her eye.

Someone moved quickly across the terrace. He paused for a second, listening, and in that second, she saw who he was. Then he was gone, disappearing into the trees.

And why, she asked herself, starting across the room, should Ken Parker be creeping about the terrace in the wee small hours?

'Where are you going?'

Her aunt's voice behind her made her jump. She whirled about, feeling guilty for being down here like this. She could not think what to say. Her face turned crimson.

'Well?' Minna demanded. 'Haven't you

anything to say? It's the middle of the night and I find you slinking about the house on tiptoe. Surely you must have some explanation?'

'I . . . I saw Dawson going out,' Ellen stammered, wishing the floor might open up and swallow her.

Her aunt had not turned on the light. It seemed strange to confront one another in the near darkness. She could not read the expression on her aunt's face.

'You must be mistaken. Dawson is in his room, asleep. When I heard you prowling around and came out to investigate, I looked in to see if he was there.'

'But I saw — '

'You thought you saw. And you were mistaken. You should be in bed. The floor is too cold to be traipsing around in your bare feet.'

'Yes, ma'am,' Ellen said disconsolately. She walked by her aunt, unable to meet her gaze directly, but she looked so pathetic that her aunt said, in a more gentle voice, 'I have some sleeping pills. Would you like to have a few? You seem to

74

be having trouble sleeping.'

'All right.'

'I'll bring them to you.'

Her aunt remained in the library. Ellen went up the stairs. There seemed little point in explaining that she was accustomed to sleeping in fits and starts. She had grown accustomed to it at Lawndale, waking after a dream, waking because a nurse had come in to look at her or take her temperature, waking because some other patient had begun screaming. If her aunt knew of her fitful sleeping she might regret having invited her to visit.

When her aunt had come and gone with the sleeping pills, Ellen still lay awake in her bed and stared at the ceiling. She had not taken the pills. She did not like to feel that control of her mind had been taken out of her hands. She had felt that way for a time, and she did not want to feel it again.

It was happening anyway, though, wasn't it? How could she say she had control of her mind and her thoughts, when she could no longer trust her senses? What did these things mean?

The boat was gone. She had checked that when she had first come back to her room. Had it ever been there? Had she seen Dawson stealing down the stairs? Or had they only been elements of another dream? And if so, when had the dream ended?

Was she still asleep, still dreaming? If so, then Minna's insistence that Dawson was in bed asleep was part of the dream too.

She was going in circles. She did not know what to believe. Fear, fear of herself, of what was happening to her mind, was like the living presence within her, moving through the corners of her consciousness, waiting for her to sleep, so that it could have control of her.

She got out of bed and went to the little writing table, switching on the light. She got paper and pen from the drawer, and began to compose a letter.

'Dear Dr. Hansen,' it began.

After a moment, she read what she had written and very precisely she tore the letter in half, and then in half again, and crumpled the pieces and threw them into the little wastebasket. She was not yet ready for that. She might have to call it quits, but not yet.

★　★　★

'There are stories of a phantom ship. People say they have seen it tied up at the landing below.' Dawson spread jam on his toast. He had, uninvited, brought up the house's ghostly history.

Ellen spilled coffee into her saucer. Had he read her mind? How did he know about the boat she had seen, or thought she saw, the night before? She had not mentioned that to her aunt. She did not think that she had, she corrected herself. But the truth was, she was no longer entirely sure what she did remember, and what she did not remember.

Minna said, 'Ellen thinks she saw you creeping around the house in the middle of the night.' She went on to tell Dawson of hearing sounds, of coming to investigate, and finding Ellen in the library.

Dawson looked amused. He turned to

Ellen and asked, 'What did you think you saw me doing?'

'Nothing,' she said warily. 'It was just a dream.'

She was afraid, afraid of what would be done if they knew how confused she was. She would not speak of these things again and somehow she would learn to separate the false from the true. She would do this because she did not want to go back to Lawndale.

But how to know what to believe? How did other people, normal people, know when they saw reality?

★ ★ ★

After breakfast, Minna thought they might want to go for a drive. 'It will do you good to get out of the house,' she told Ellen. 'Dawson, would you like to join us?'

'I think not. I have some work to do on my manuscript. Anyway, Pomfret's driving is not my idea of first class travel.'

'Nonsense. Pomfret is perfectly capable, it's those other drivers who cause all the problems.'

With this pronouncement, she went in search of the elder servant to instruct him to have the car brought around. A vintage Packard, it was waiting when Minna and Ellen came out a few minutes later. Pomfret, wearing a chauffeur's cap at a jaunty angle, held the door for them.

As they drove very slowly along the terrace, Minna named the inhabitants of the houses they passed. She seemed to weigh each of them in the balance, and find them wanting.

'The Creightons live there,' she said, pointing. 'They have the yellow cottage you can see through the trees, although they rent it out. You won't like Mrs. Creighton at all. She's wishy-washy.'

A smart looking woman came out the front door of a house down the street. Minna nodded to her in passing, and the woman gave a slight nod in return.

'Mrs. Clark. Frankly, she came from a common background, but she took Mr. Clark away from his first wife, and all his money to boot. And she's been well trained. You'd really think to talk to her that she was from a good family.'

'Do you like her?'

Minna's eyes gleamed. 'She's clever, I'll give her that. Of course it's not right to steal another woman's husband, but she is a good wife to him, no one can fault her in that respect. And she didn't skulk around to do it, either, she came right out in the open and took what she wanted. You can't call her wishy-washy.'

She said this last with pure venom. Ellen made a mental note to be definite in her dealings with her aunt. It seemed it was all right to engage in villainy that had the courage of its convictions, but vacillation was not to be tolerated.

Aunt Minna leaned back a little against the dark upholstery. 'Have you got a young man?'

Ellen blushed and stammered, 'No, I haven't.'

Miller gave her a penetrating look. 'Why not? You're pretty enough. Not like I was at your age, but pretty anyway.'

'The problem is, no young man has seemed to share your opinion.'

Minna took a moment to digest this information. When she spoke again it was to say, to Ellen's further surprise, 'I had a young man.'

'Did you?'

'You needn't sound that surprised. He was quite handsome. Literally begged me on bended knee to marry him. And I almost did. The trouble was, he was too opinionated, and wanted me to share his opinions. Always telling me what to do, and what to say, even what to think. Tried to get me to vote Republican once. I knew then that it would never do. But it never came to that point anyway. He died.'

'How sad.'

'An automobile accident. Banged him up badly. He cried and wanted me by him at the end. The really sad thing is, when I saw him in that hospital bed, all hurt and helpless, I actually did want to marry him. In all the time I'd known him, that was the first he'd really inspired any emotion in me. But it was too late, of course. He died, without ever knowing I changed my mind.'

She put a parchment-like hand on Ellen's. 'They're all like that, really. Don't be misled by appearances. They may look healthy and strong, but underneath they're all helpless creatures.'

They rode in silence for a block or two, Pomfret handling the car cautiously. He did not seem particularly at ease in the traffic and Ellen thought probably they did not often go out driving.

'Savannah is a lovely city,' Ellen said.

'Yes,' Minna agreed, sounding pleased that her niece should think so. 'I would love to have seen it before the war. It must have been splendid.'

'Didn't you see it then? I somehow thought the family had been here quite a while.'

'The war ended in Eighteen Sixty-five,' Minna said in a voice sharp with annoyance. 'I am not that old.'

Ellen realized her mistake at once. 'You mean the Civil War. I thought you meant World War Two.'

'That was nothing,' Minna said, dismissing it with a wave of her hand. 'All in Europe. No one fired a shot in Savannah.' She chuckled at some memory, going in a twinkling from bad humor to good. 'Your mother was here then, and from the way she shook in her boots, you'd have thought the Hessians were in the city firing on the houses. One time there was a raid, with the sirens blowing, and the lights blacked out, you know. They seemed to think we would be bombed.

'I got dressed and sat in my room, but when it was all over, we found that your mother had rushed down to the basement in her nightdress, and sat with the servants. Of course, if we have them again, air raids I mean, you must do as you wish.'

It was quite clear to Ellen that in the unlikely event such raids should happen again, she had better not be found in the basement if she meant to win her aunt's favor.

Minna's mind seemed to skip unfettered from one subject to another. It went back to the earlier discussion now as easily as if they had not ended it. She said in a sad voice, 'You mustn't wait until you're old to marry. Don't think because you're young you can go on picking and choosing. It's better to have someone, even the wrong someone. No one knows what loneliness is until it's too late.'

Ellen was startled by this sudden change in the usually stern manner of the woman beside her. Some haunting memory had wrought a change in her aunt. The grandeur had seemed all at once to flee, and left in its wake a gaunt gray figure, rustling the dead leaves of the past.

'But surely you'll never be lonely,' Ellen said, and impetuously threw an arm about her aunt's shoulders. Minna's smile returned, and for a brief instant Ellen could see that she must indeed have been lovely once.

'You're a good person,' Minna said, patting her cheek. 'I'm glad you've come, regardless.' She did not say regardless of what, but Ellen thought she could finish the sentence: 'Regardless of your mental condition.'

But she thought too that in one sense, her coming had been a blessing for her aunt, and that gave her some comfort. She felt that here she might be needed and useful, if only to dispel her aunt's loneliness.

Later, Pomfret brought them back and deposited them outside number fourteen. Aunt Minna alighted first. Her inquisitive eyes swept the street, and found a source of interest.

'Who's that walking?'

Ellen, getting out of the car, was turned the wrong way, but Minna quickly answered her own question. 'It's Mr. Parker. But who is the young lady he's walking with?'

Ellen had an inkling of what she would see before she even looked. She had an intuitive knowledge that young Mr. Parker's head would not be turned by any ordinary beauty, and certainly not by a face as plain as her own.

It was indeed Mr. Parker. At the moment he was engaged in conversation, and seemingly enchanted with, a woman every bit as beautiful as Ellen had feared. She was tall and carried her head of rich golden hair like a queen. In her hand was a double lead by which she managed two golden retrievers who walked with their own elegant grace. It was a picture out of a magazine advertisement.

Ellen was surprised to discover how immediately resentful she was of the other woman. She had not met her yet, true, but there was no need. She already knew what she was like. Or at any rate she knew what she was not like.

Certainly she was not a woman who had needed a year at a mental hospital and at whom people as a result still looked a bit askance. She had all the dignity, poise, and grace any man would naturally look for in a woman.

Ellen would have liked to make an escape, but Mr. Parker waved at them in a manner that indicated he wanted them to wait. He said something aside to his lovely companion, something amusing, which made her laugh.

He opened the door of a brilliant red convertible for her and she got gracefully in, leaning forward so the dogs could leap into the rear seat. She and Mr. Parker exchanged some final words, and he left her. Long before he had reached Ellen and Minna, the blonde in the red convertible had pulled away and was out of sight, driving fast, and taking a corner with tires squealing a protest.

Ellen tried, in that eternity while he walked toward them, to think what she should say and how she should act.

He smiled brightly and, looking completely at ease, said, 'Hello.'

She could think of nothing to say. She knew both he and her aunt were watching her, making her the center of attention. She must say something, anything.

She heard a voice which could only be hers saying, 'Mr. Parker, I thought I saw you on our back terrace last night.'

He took half a step back as if she had slapped him, and said, 'Lord, we aren't going through that sort of thing again, are we?'

Minna's eyebrows went up disapprovingly. Ellen stood in anguish, not wanting to go on, and unable to go back.

She said, 'I am sorry, now that I see you again, I realize I was mistaken.' As soon as she had said it she saw how stupid that made her seem.

Minna, however, was not so easily disconcerted. 'Were you on our terrace last night?'

He laughed. Her icy question seemed to restore the good humor that Ellen had dissipated.

'No. Scout's honor. And what I really came for was to ask Miss Ellen if she's seen our little park yet?'

'No,' Ellen replied quietly.

'Then may I show it to you? To both of you, of course,' he added, tossing Minna a flashing grin.

'I've seen it. I've been living by our little park for a number of years. But of course, Ellen must do as she wishes.'

'I would enjoy seeing it,' Ellen said, loath to refuse his invitation, and yet not wanting to annoy her aunt. 'Do you mind, Aunt?'

Minna's manner softened abruptly. 'Go along, dear, but don't go farther than the iron fence. I read in the newspapers that the streets are not safe anymore.'

She went in, leaving Ellen with Ken on the sidewalk. He offered her his arm. 'Shall we?'

She took it, and together they crossed the street into the little park. It was just a few trees, some grass with a path winding through it, and one old wrought iron bench. It all had a neglected look that told more pointedly than words how the neighborhood had changed from what it once had been.

But there was a charm to any stretch of greenery and open space. She strolled with him along the path, thinking just now that the park was truly breathtaking.

'You mustn't mind my aunt,' she said. 'She's very sweet, but a little old-fashioned.'

'Yes. One is safe if one stays within the iron fences.' They had reached the fence, once painted white, but now turned to rust. He ran his fingers along the row of spires.

'That may have been true, once.'

He looked at her intently. 'Where do you feel safe?'

'I'm not sure that feeling safe is the ultimate, actually. I mean, I was some-place recently where I did feel safe, utterly safe, but a bird in a cage is safe, don't you see? Life is dangerous and uncertain and the less of life we're exposed to, the safer we are. But you don't really succeed in having more life. You only have less of it for longer.'

He was thinking, *I'm wasting time with this conversation. I ought to be questioning her, seeing what I can pry out of her. That's what I am here for. That's why I coaxed her to come over here with me.*

'I feel completely safe just now,' she said. 'Here, with you.'

And how was he to interrogate her after a remark like that?

He took her arm, a bit roughly. 'Come on, I'd better get you back before your aunt starts watching us with that telescope of hers.'

She found she almost had to run to keep up with his long strides. That she had said the wrong thing again was painfully obvious. He was angry. She felt humiliated, without knowing exactly why.

At the steps leading to number fourteen, he said, roughly, 'You shouldn't be here, in Savannah.'

She had already started up the steps, and paused to turn around and look down into his face. 'I had no place else to go.'

He turned on his heel and left without even saying goodbye. He walked quickly, purposefully. She went numb, feeling a little dazed by his behavior, and hurt, and puzzled. Why should he have gotten angry?

6

Aunt Minna's loneliness was brought home to Ellen the following evening. After dinner, Minna said, 'I'm afraid you'll be on your own tonight. Dawson and I have an errand we must run, and you won't be able to come with us.'

Dawson quickly added, 'You'd only be bored. We're calling on some old ladies who have houses I want to research for my book. You know the sort of thing it will be, sherry and biscuits, and much talk of when father was alive.'

'I wonder how you talk about evenings with me, when I'm not around,' Minna said.

To ward off any impending argument, Ellen said, 'I don't mind. I've got some letters to write, and it'll be nice to curl up with a book.'

Dawson and Minna went out soon after dinner. Ellen observed that Minna had dressed for the evening and looked, if not lovely, certainly regal in a dress of deep purple, and with it a splendid amethyst and diamond brooch.

Dinner was always early, as the two women servants, Bertha and Mrs. Bondage, left as soon as it had been cleared. Pomfret's rooms were in the basement, and he disappeared with the setting sun.

For all practical purposes, Ellen had the house to herself. She did not much mind. Alone, she need not be afraid of saying the wrong thing, something that might reflect on her judgment.

She wrote a letter to her mother, a noncommittal note that talked much and said little. She would have liked to talk frankly to someone, but there was no one to whom she could bare her soul. Her mother would only fly into a panic. Dr. Hansen would ponder the matter mightily, and suggest another stay at Lawndale. Minna was out of the question. In the end, she was on her own.

She was re-reading *War and Peace*, and for a time she traveled happily through Tolstoy's Russia.

The clock struck nine, bringing her

back to Savannah and the present. She was accustomed to retiring early, another legacy from Lawndale. She went up to her room and prepared for bed, but she realized she had left her book in the library and went down for it.

The house was still. The stairs creaked, revealing their age. She had an uneasy feeling that she could not quite identify, as if she expected something to happen. The clock struck the quarter hour. Its chimes echoed through the house, hovering in the quiet air.

She stopped dead just inside the library door. Across from her a man pressed his face against the glass of the large French doors, peering in.

He saw her. For a second or so they stood frozen, staring at one another. Her first thought was that it was Ken, but, no, this man was a stranger, a Latino. She saw that much in the few seconds before he left, so quickly that she could almost believe she had imagined him.

Her legs were unsteady and her throat felt dry. Another figment of her imagination, or real? She fought down her fear.

No, he had been real, she was sure of that. And there were countless reasons, perfectly harmless ones, why he might have been there. She went to the French doors. Her hand shook as she slid back the bolt and pulled one of them open.

'Hello.' She stepped onto the terrace. The only reply was a rustling in the trees that was surely the leaves in the wind.

Back inside, she bolted the door again. Her book was where she had left it, on the chair, but she hadn't the heart to go upstairs now, leaving the downstairs empty. She had no idea how sound a sleeper Pomfret was, or if he would hear her if she should yell. She told herself that if she really thought the man had been a prowler, she should call the police.

But a fear more urgent than any fear of prowlers held her back. She did not dare begin acting like a frightened neurotic, jumping at shadows, calling the police willy-nilly. Anyone might look into the woods at night and think they saw someone there — or think they saw a face in a dark window. But Aunt Minna already thought she was imagining things.

She turned the lights out and, turning her back on the French doors, curled up in a chair to wait for her aunt to come in. She meant to stay awake, but she fell asleep.

She woke to the sound of the front door closing. 'Try to be quiet,' Aunt Minna's voice said. 'We don't want to disturb Ellen.'

Dawson made some reply in a low voice she couldn't hear.

'It's all right,' Ellen called, stretching and getting out of the chair. 'I'm in here.'

The moonlight turned Minna's hair to bright silver. On her face was a look Ellen hadn't seen before, a look such as a young woman might wear coming from a tryst with her lover.

'Heavens, what are you doing in here, in the dark?' Minna asked.

'I couldn't sleep. Or I thought I couldn't, but I must have fallen asleep after all.'

'Well, come along, your bed will be welcome now, I'm sure.'

As she trailed up the stairs behind her aunt, Ellen was puzzled by her aunt's radiance. Was it possible Aunt Minna had a crush on Dawson Elliot? He was a handsome man, who must have alleviated some of her loneliness.

It was a sad possibility to contemplate. Dawson might be fond of her in his own way, but it was evident that he did not see her romantically. And when his book was finished, he would be on his way.

★   ★   ★

In her own room, Minna was brushing her hair and thinking how utterly exciting her life had become. Who would ever have dreamed that so much could be happening to her?

★   ★   ★

While Ellen slept late in the morning, Dawson and Minna quarreled over coffee.

'We've got to get her out of the house,' Dawson insisted.

'It's out of the question. I can't just send her packing. Think what it might do to her. She has no confidence as it is. She's like a frightened rabbit, afraid of her own shadow.'

Dawson sighed and lit a cigarette, ignoring her disapproval. 'Then how do you propose we get those things loaded?'

'It will have to be done late, after she's gone to sleep.'

'There's too much for that. It'll take a week loading it that way. And besides, there's no guarantee she'll stay in bed once she's gone there. Unless . . . ' He lifted an eyebrow. 'Unless we give her something.'

'No. She has some of my sleeping pills. If she feels the need for them and takes them herself, that's one thing, but I won't condone having my own niece drugged without her knowledge.'

'Then you've got to get her out of the house for a full evening. Think of something . . . '

The ringing of the phone interrupted him. Minna looked puzzled. She did not have that many telephone calls and it was still relatively early.

In a moment, Bondage appeared in the

doorway. 'It's that Mr. Parker, who lives over at the Creightons',' she said. 'He asked for Miss Ellen and when I told him she was still in bed, he asked to speak to you, ma'am.'

'There's a production of Tosca tonight, at the civic auditorium,' Ken said when Minna came to the phone, 'and I happened to have four tickets. I wondered if you and Mr. Elliot and your niece wouldn't like to join me?'

'We'd be delighted.' It was a perfect way to get Ellen out of the house. 'Absolutely delighted.'

They settled the time and the arrangements for meeting and he rang off. She was smiling when she came back into the breakfast room.

'What did he want?' Dawson asked.

'You needn't sound so grumpy.' She really did not like the peremptory tone Dawson sometimes used with her, and it pleased her to be a little obstinate.

He gave her an icy look but her spirits were too good to continue to tease him. 'He wants to take us to the opera. I accepted for Ellen and myself. So you will have a free hand for the evening.'

'That,' he said, looking pleased, 'will make things much easier.'

★　★　★

Ken replaced the phone on its cradle and turned to the blonde stretched out on the divan. 'All set,' he said. 'I'll see that they're away from the house for the evening. The rest is up to you.'

Maggie Shaffer got up from the sofa and stretched. She wore a plain skirt and sweater, but she managed to look as glamorous and beautiful in them as she had when Ellen had seen her dressed in tweeds. She gave an impression of background and wealth and breeding.

Most people who met her thought she came from upper New York State, from a moneyed, conservative family. In fact, she came from a very poor farm in the Georgia heartland. She'd had to work her way through high school and hadn't finished college, but she had discovered early on that she had a gift for mimicry.

'Don't worry,' she said, 'if there's

anything hidden in that house, I'll find it. Just keep them away for a couple of hours, at least.'

'We'd better have a signal, in case. If anything comes up, I'll dial the Miles house and let the phone ring once. That means you're to hightail it. Do not pass go, do not collect two hundred dollars, just beat it.'

'Will do. Are you meeting them here?'

'No, I didn't want to risk their seeing you. We're meeting at Bolton's Restaurant. That'll give you an extra hour or so.'

* * *

Ellen felt as if she were dressing for the prom. She had already changed dresses three times and was even now studying her reflection in the mirror with a critical look. She looked chic and ultra-feminine in the black cocktail dress.

Her aunt was in her dressing room. With help from Bondage, she was just getting into an old-fashioned but still elegant gown of gray silk.

'Quit fussing, Bondage,' she snapped

when Ellen came in. 'Let me see, dear. Hmm, very pretty. But you need something. Let me think. Yes, that will be perfect. Go in and look in the jewel case atop my bureau. There's a diamond and onyx brooch that will work nicely.'

Ellen found the jewel case, but she did not see the brooch Aunt Minna had described. There were papers in the case and she picked them up to see if the brooch was under them. She saw with surprise that the papers were pawn tickets.

'Did you find it?' Aunt Minna called.

'It doesn't seem to be here.' Ellen quickly put the pawn tickets back into the box.

'Nonsense, it must . . . oh.' Minna bustled into the room, Bondage hurrying after her. 'Never mind about that one,' she said, snatching up the jewel box. 'This will do better.' She took a delicate pendant from atop the dresser.

'Are these real?' Ellen asked, putting it about her neck. The stones appeared to be emeralds and diamonds. They looked gorgeous against the black of her dress.

'You surely don't imagine I have imitations,' Aunt Minna said in an indignant tone.

'But, shouldn't they be in a vault?' Minna gave a disdainful snort. 'It's certainly lovely,' Ellen said, fingering the pendant.

'Yes, it will do. Now go wait in the sitting room and Bondage will bring you some tea.'

'Begging your pardon, ma'am,' Bondage said, trying to get a scarf properly attached to the silk gown, 'but you wanted me to help you dress.'

'I'm not incompetent,' Minna snapped, snatching the scarf from Bondage's hands. 'Now fetch some tea for Ellen, go on.'

She shooed them both out of the room. Bondage went after tea and Ellen sat stiffly on the little, hard settee and thought about the pawn tickets she'd discovered.

Her aunt must be selling her jewelry to raise money. That must mean, she thought with a horrible surge of guilt, that her visit had been too great a financial burden.

No sooner had this thought occurred to her than she saw what nonsense it was. She had hardly been a financial burden since she'd come here. Granted, another mouth to feed meant extra expense, but surely not enough to warrant selling jewelry worth, judging from what she had seen, many thousands of dollars.

Her aunt had obviously wanted to raise a considerable sum of money for some reason other than her niece's visit. Perhaps her style of living, with or without Ellen here, was more than she could afford. Servants, a big old house — it wasn't a frugal lifestyle.

A new thought popped into her mind. Maybe she did not ordinarily live as she did now. Maybe it was Dawson's coming to live with her that had played havoc with her finances. Was Aunt Minna living in an extravagant manner to impress Dawson?

Which, of course, was none of her business. But she must do something to help. Her own finances were not lavish but she was not in dire straits, either. She would insist upon making a contribution to the household expenses.

If Minna was worried about money, however, or anything else, she did not show it when she joined Ellen shortly. At a glance it looked as if she had emptied the jewel box of all its remaining contents. On someone else the results might have been vulgar, but on her the abundance of jewelry seemed somehow appropriate. She looked very much the *grande dame*, and very excited about their evening.

'I haven't been to an opera in more years than I can remember,' she said, leading the way downstairs. 'We're going to have a splendid time, I just know it.'

It was impossible not to share her enthusiasm, and Ellen forgot to worry. She had almost never been on a date, though she wasn't sure if this qualified as one or not. In any case, she couldn't not be excited at the prospect of spending an evening with Ken Parker, even with Aunt Minna as chaperone.

Dawson was in the hall as they came down. He gave a low whistle, looking from one to the other. 'I'm sorry now I can't join you,' he said. 'You're going to turn every head in the place.'

'Why don't you join us?' Ellen asked. In her expansive mood, she could even feel friendly toward Dawson.

'Alas, the writer's lot is not a happy one. Editors are cruel taskmasters. I shall have to settle for your full reports when you return.'

As they were going out, he said, 'Enjoy yourselves. Don't hurry home.'

⋆　⋆　⋆

Ken rose smiling to greet them when the maître d' led them to his table, but his smile faded when he looked past Ellen's shoulders. 'Where's Dawson?' he asked.

'Mr. Elliot was not able to make it this evening,' Minna said. 'He sends his apologies.'

'I see.' There was an odd and awkward silence before Ken recovered his manners. 'Please, sit down.'

He held a chair for Minna and then for Ellen. Ellen had an impression that he was more disappointed than he ought to have been by Dawson's absence. She could see that he must have a fourth ticket for the opera, which would probably be wasted, but surely it wasn't all that serious. Probably he could find someone outside the auditorium to take it off his hands.

He ordered a sherry for Minna and a gimlet for Ellen. When the waiter had gone, he said, 'Will you excuse me for a minute. I have to make a phone call.'

He cursed himself silently as he made his way through the crowded dining room. He knew what Nielsen would say — he had been careless in not determining that Dawson would be here. He had taken it for granted, but he had been in this business long enough to know you couldn't get guarantees on these things. You made plans, and hoped things developed in accordance with them, but the best laid plans of mice and men, and so on.

There was no answer at his cottage, so Maggie had already left. He dialed the Miles' number, keeping one finger on the

107

disconnect button. It rang once and he disconnected.

That was it. If Maggie was there already, she had been warned. But it was also possible she wasn't yet there. She might have gone out to dinner herself, or she might be in transit between the two places. He would have to make certain by repeating the warning a little later.

Watching him return to the table, Ellen saw through her own veil of happiness that something was worrying him. He sat down, smiled at her, and the conversation moved along smoothly. He ordered dinner, to Minna's apparent pleasure. But something was amiss.

Throughout the dinner, Ellen saw that he was not completely with them. Part of his mind was somewhere else. When he inadvertently called her Maggie, she thought she understood. As if through psychic revelation, she knew that Maggie was the elegant blonde with the retrievers.

She studied the worried look in his eyes when he thought she wasn't watching him, and decided that he must have quarreled with Maggie. That would explain the phone call — he was trying to patch things up, or perhaps arranging to meet later, after he had gotten rid of his present company.

Ellen's mood of bright joy faded. She had to force herself to keep up her end of the conversation. Food that had tasted delicious a moment before was now like sawdust in her mouth.

It was nearly curtain time when they arrived at the auditorium and the lobby was filled with the cream of the city's society. Ellen was surprised to see how many people greeted her aunt. Minna seemed a bit surprised herself.

'They remember me,' she said in a whisper. 'They don't like me, but they can't forget me either. The Miles name matters here, girl. Remember that.'

'Excuse me for a moment,' Ken said. 'I'll be right back.'

Another phone call, Ellen thought. To Maggie.

Aunt Minna knew that her niece was being very quiet, but in her own high spirits she just supposed Ellen was awed by this exposure to the city's elite. In whispers, she pointed out members of the local establishment as they entered the lobby.

'The Whites,' she whispered, pointing out a handsome couple just entering through the main doorway. 'Those pearls are fake.'

The Whites came by to greet Minna and be introduced to Ellen. Ellen could not help taking a closer look at the pearls. They looked genuine to her, but she did not for a moment doubt that her aunt was right.

When the Whites had gone, Minna indicated another couple. 'The Burtons. She's sweet to her husband in public but I'm told she's having an affair with her gardener. Can you imagine, a gardener?'

Through the crowd, Ellen caught a glimpse of Ken on his cellphone across the room.

7

At that moment, Maggie was nowhere near a telephone. She was in her convertible, in the fast lane, and not moving at all. The traffic was bumper-to-bumper and stopped cold. Ahead, she could see the red glow of an emergency vehicle. Obviously there had been a wreck — a pretty bad one, it seemed. She had been sitting where she was for twenty minutes already. She could only hope that soon the road would be cleared and traffic would start moving again.

She lit a cigarette and tried to talk herself out of her impatience. They would be at the opera for a long while yet. She was losing time, true, but not so much. If the traffic started to move soon, everything would still be all right.

★ ★ ★

The opera was Tosca, high melodrama filled with exciting music. Ellen tried to lose herself in the performance. Beside her, Ken fidgeted, glancing often at his watch. She could almost feel a current of tension emanating from him, greater even than the tension on the stage.

She was sorry she had come. She felt sure he would rather be with Maggie, and that thought was like a knife stabbing her.

She thought surely he would telephone again during the intermission, but to her surprise, he did not. They had a drink in the bar. People around them talked about the first act. Their little trio seemed to have run out of conversation.

During the dramatic second act, Ellen tried to forget her own unhappiness, and focus on the happenings onstage, but the soprano reminded her of Maggie, glamorous and aristocratic.

★　★　★

Just at the moment, Maggie Shaffer did not look particularly aristocratic or glamorous. She had finally escaped from the traffic jam, rushing back to Ken's place to change into her 'work clothes'. When she came down the path from the cottage a few minutes later, she was all in black — black stretch pants, black jersey, even a black scarf that covered her blonde hair.

She was late. She would have to work fast when she got into the house.

She approached the Miles house from the back terrace and saw that lights were on inside. She supposed the occupants had left them on when they went out. It made her work a little more risky, but not much. She would be visible while she got the French doors open, but there was little chance that someone was likely to be strolling past back here and see her.

She paused at the edge of the terrace, some instinctive warning stirring at the back of her mind. Ken had promised to have everyone out of the house. The two servant women left early and the old man was driving the car. Elliot, Minna and her niece should be in it.

By all rights she should have nothing to worry about. Still, for a full five minutes she remained in the shadow of a big, old oak tree, watching the lighted French doors and the library beyond them. Nothing stirred.

Finally she stole across the terrace. She tried the French doors automatically. Sometimes people forgot to lock up, but the occupants had not. She took a set of picks from her shoulder bag, and in a moment she had the door open.

She closed it softly after herself and took quick stock of her surroundings. It was unlikely anything really interesting would be here. The sort of thing she was looking for would be hidden, in a bedroom, perhaps, or the attic.

The upstairs rooms were the most dangerous. If anyone should come home while she was searching, she would be trapped. So she would start at the top, the attic, and work her way down.

She was almost to the head of the stairs when she heard a sound. Could that have been the opening of a door? She glanced down. If the occupants came home, they would almost certainly come in by the front door, and it was still closed. Anyway, it was far too early.

* * *

'How exciting,' Ellen said, enthusiastically applauding the performers as they came out to take their bows after the second act. 'Didn't you enjoy it?'

'Hmm? Oh, yes, very nice,' Ken said. 'Look, I'm sorry, I'm going to try my phone call again. I'll join you in the lobby.' Without waiting for a reply, he was gone, pushing his way through the crowd in the aisles.

He was probably being overly cautious. Maggie had likely heard his signal before. Still, it wouldn't hurt to give it again. It had not been much after dark when he called before. No doubt she would have waited for darkness to descend.

Ken stopped at the restroom. By the time he got back to the lobby, a buzzer was already warning that the next act was about to begin. Ken took his cell phone from his pocket and hit redial, waiting for the single ring. Then, hurrying, he hit the disconnect button, slipped the phone into his pocket, and went back inside.

He was too quick to hear the man's voice that answered the phone's ring. 'Hello?' it said sharply.

The music had begun by the time Ken slipped into place beside Ellen. She couldn't tell if he were still so worried or not. She tried to concentrate on the opera.

★ ★ ★

Maggie had reached the upstairs hall when the phone shrilled. In the split second that followed, she knew the second ring was too long in coming. It was Ken, warning her to get out. She dived for the stairs again — and heard the click of a telephone receiver being lifted, and a man's voice said, impatiently, 'Hello?'

She had moved too fast. She saw him now at the foot of the stairs — and he saw her. He put the telephone slowly back into place, his eyes locked on hers. She knew he was Elliot, and she knew too that of all the people who might have been here, he was potentially the most dangerous. She had a gun in her shoulder bag. She smiled at him in a flirtatious manner and said, 'I think I can explain. I have something here to show you . . . '

She reached for her bag but he was quicker. He drew a revolver from inside his jacket and aimed it up the stairs at her.

'Don't move,' he said.

★   ★   ★

Ken had done all he could do. He had given Maggie the warning signal three times. Now he could take it for granted that she had gotten the message. He could relax and enjoy the evening and the lovely young woman beside him.

Only she did not seem to be enjoying the evening. Not that he could blame her, the way he'd been hopping up and down, making telephone calls.

The last act ended and the curtain fell.

Ellen applauded enthusiastically. Ken put a hand lightly on her arm and said,

'I'm sorry to have neglected you.'

'It's all right,' she said stiffly. 'I've enjoyed the opera.'

'I haven't.'

She turned, surprised, to look at him. The house lights had come up and she saw by their glare how strained he looked. Something was worrying him, really worrying him. His concern touched a responsive chord in her. She wanted to help him, to ease whatever burden he was carrying. She did not see what a change in roles this meant for her — she, who for months had badly needed the comfort of others, was eager now to give comfort.

'It's kept me from looking at you,' he said, smiling. Some of the tension faded from his face when he smiled.

'Tell you what,' he said when they were on the sidewalk outside, the crowd of opera-goers thinning about them, 'let's go somewhere for a late snack and a drink.'

'I think not,' Minna said. She looked radiantly happy, Ellen thought, realizing how much her aunt had enjoyed this evening out; but she looked tired too.

Ken was disappointed. 'I was counting

on making a night of it. It isn't often I get to escort two charming ladies.'

Minna tried not to be pleased by the flattery, but she obviously was. 'Nevertheless, I am quite sleepy and if I don't get started now, I expect Pomfret will fall asleep before he gets me home. So you shall have to be content with one charming lady, Mr. Parker.'

Ellen had assumed her aunt would expect her to come home with her. 'I don't know,' she said doubtfully.

'Don't you try to desert me too,' Ken said. He was remembering that he had promised to keep them out as late as possible. But it couldn't make much difference if Minna went home now. By this time Maggie was probably long gone from the house.

He looked so sincere that Ellen said, 'If you don't mind, Aunt Minna.'

'Nonsense.' Minna patted her shoulder. 'Go along with Mr. Parker and have some fun. It will do you a world of good. It isn't healthy for a young thing like you to be cooped up all the time in a musty old house with an old woman for company.'

Pomfret had driven up in the Packard and Minna got into the car. 'Don't bring her home before dawn,' she said, and the big old car pulled away into the stream of traffic.

'Well,' Ken said, signaling for a cab, 'let's go back and pick up my car. Have you any preferences? We've got . . . ' he glanced at his watch, 'about seven hours.'

'Seven hours?'

'Until dawn.'

★   ★   ★

Afterward, Ellen could hardly keep the details of that night clear in her mind. They seemed to blur into one great rosy glow.

It was a lovely night, on that point she was clear. His car was a convertible, the top down. She put her stole over her head and leaned back in the seat to watch the sky aswarm with stars, and the moon that slipped in and out between the buildings. Her heart felt as if it were up there among the stars, soaring skyward in a burst of freedom.

They talked as if they had always known one another. He asked about her home life and for the first time she found herself talking about it easily and frankly. She could even tell him about Lawndale, not with regret but as if it were amusing, even pleasant.

If he talked less than she, she did not mind.

They went to another restaurant, less grand than the earlier one. He seemed to be a familiar face there. The head waiter greeted them enthusiastically and gave them a good table, although the room was crowded.

They ate a light supper and danced to a smooth, old-fashioned sounding band. She loved the feel of his arms about her, and thought she could die happily just then.

Later they drove through the nearly deserted streets of Savannah. He drove fast but well. The long, low-slung sports car seemed to be an extension of his will. Ellen felt happier than she had ever been.

They reached the street that wound its way up to the terrace, and went by it.

'Isn't that our street?' she asked.

'I know of a place. It's just a little illegal. I thought it would be fun to go there.' He looked aside at her. 'Do you mind?'

'No.' After a moment she laughed aloud.

'What's so funny?'

'I was just thinking, what if they raid this slightly illegal place? Can you imagine what Minna would say if you and I got arrested in some den of iniquity?'

He laughed too, thinking rather of what Nielsen would say.

They left the city. After a bit, he turned off the main highway onto a narrow country road. They came to what appeared to be a large but otherwise ordinary farmhouse. Lights showed in the windows.

'What do they do here, anyway?' she asked as they turned into the gravel drive.

'It's mostly gambling. There's more to it than that, but not anything you'd be interested in.'

The noise level inside was high. They came into a hall thick with smoke and the sound of raucous voices. Two women in skimpy dresses sat on barstools against the wall — no doubt what Ken had referred to that she would not be interested in.

A small dance floor, crowded with couples, opened off the hall they were in. In other rooms patrons, mostly men, gambled. He had to explain blackjack to her and then she played for him, and won. It was something she had never imagined herself doing and she felt actually giddy with excitement.

They had coffee and brandy in the bar, and laughed because they felt like they were without a care in the world.

By the time they finally drove home, practically no one was stirring. Ken walked her from the place where he parked his car back to Minna's. She might have been floating on a cloud. She was sleepy and wide awake all at the same time. At the door, she thanked him for a wonderful evening and said good night, wondering if he would kiss her.

He hesitated for a long moment, as if considering it. 'Tell your aunt I kept my promise,' he said, and started down the steps. The sky was growing light with dawn.

She climbed to her room in a daze. She was only dimly conscious of undressing and getting into bed. She was drunk, but not from the wine and the brandy.

She was utterly, hopelessly in love with Ken Parker.

8

She woke feeling light-headed. Memories of the night before flooded into her mind. She wriggled her toes and savored the recollections.

With a little laugh of happiness, she got out of bed and dressed. The house was quiet when she came down. There was no sign of either Dawson or Aunt Minna. She rang for Bertha and when she came, asked if she could have some breakfast.

'Right away, miss.' Bertha gave her a conspiratorial smile. 'Your aunt thought you might sleep late. We've been keeping breakfast ready for you. I hope you had a pleasant night.'

'I did, thank you.'

'I said to Bondage, that girl deserves a little fun, after all she's been through.' She gave a cluck of her tongue and went off to get breakfast ready.

Ellen tried not to let her spirits droop. It was to be expected that the servants would know her history, but it was a bit discouraging nonetheless. Would she ever live her past down and be done with it, really done with it?

Bertha brought in breakfast on a tray — coffee, toast, fruit and a warm omelet. Ellen discovered she was very hungry indeed and set to the food with gusto.

'Your aunt had some shopping to do,' Bertha said when she brought more coffee. 'I was to tell you so you wouldn't worry.'

'And Mr. Elliot, is he out also?'

'Yes, ma'am, he went out early.' Bertha's bright smile always faded when she spoke of Dawson. Ellen had the impression the servants didn't much care for Mr. Elliot, although he seemed pleasant enough to them when Ellen was around.

Perhaps, Ellen thought, they too suspected he had a place to which he was not quite entitled in her aunt's affections. Bertha and Bondage and Pomfret were all long-time employees and no doubt they felt some loyalty for their employer. Minna could be crotchety, but they seemed to take it in good stride. In most respects their jobs were enviable, not too difficult and well paid.

Yet, she too felt an inexplicable dislike for him, even knowing she was being unfair. He had always been charming and polite toward her. If anything, maybe too much so.

She had brought the emerald and diamond pendant downstairs with her, to return it to Aunt Minna. It reminded her of the pawn tickets in her aunt's jewel case. They were a different matter. She would not interfere in her aunt's personal business, but finances were another matter. Something was amiss in that realm, clearly, and she ought to do what she could to help.

The trouble was, she did not know what she could do, or how to do anything without offending her aunt.

Breakfast over, she let herself out of the house and took the path that led through the trees. She told herself she had no destination in mind, but when she came to the clearing, she knew where she wanted to go. She wanted to see Ken again.

She knew a woman was not supposed to show herself so interested. But at the thought of him, her heart sang and she took the path that went up to his cottage. There was no harm in thanking him again for a lovely evening. She needn't wear her heart on her sleeve. This would be a neighborly gesture, nothing more.

The cottage was smaller than she had realized from a distance. She knocked at the door, feeling a bit timid now that she was here.

He did not answer the door at once and she began to think maybe he was out. When he did open the door finally, however, looking surprised to see her, he had a phone to his ear. He mouthed a silent greeting, motioning her in, and said, into the phone, 'Oh, sure.'

She looked around with ill-concealed curiosity. There wasn't much to see. It was an empty room — not devoid of furnishing but empty in the way a rented room is inevitably empty.

Two studio beds were arranged in an L, with a lamp in the corner on a triangular table. A big easy chair, battered and comfortable-looking, sat near the window. A desk, by which Ken stood just now, and a dresser, made up the rest of the furnishings. Through a doorway to the left she could see a counter top and a kitchen sink, and at the other side a stubby dressing room led to a bathroom. The mirror in the hall gave her almost a full view of the bathroom and a closet with its doors ajar — a closet with a blue silk dress on a hanger.

In her mind's eye she could see the blue silk on the elegant blonde, Maggie. She saw herself, drab in comparison. She curled up inside herself in an agony of embarrassment, wishing she hadn't come.

Ken was still on the phone. She could still escape. She threw him an apologetic look and moved toward the door. He clapped a hand over the mouthpiece.

'Wait,' he said.

He finished his conversation and hung up. 'Well,' he said, 'to what do I owe this unexpected pleasure?'

She could all but hear Aunt Minna's disdainful snort. 'I came to thank you for last night,' she stammered, feeling like a wayward child.

'I should thank you. The pleasure was all mine.'

'Oh, no, not at all,' she blurted out without thinking. She blushed and said, 'I've got to go.'

She fled without waiting for his reply, grateful for the shelter of the trees into which she ran. He came to the door, looking after her, puzzled.

She took the path that went down to the water. She did not want to see anyone just now. She had made a fool of herself, again. How could she have been so stupid? She had let herself exaggerate the importance of a few pleasant words, a few smooth dances.

She leaned on the rough-textured wooden rail that ran along one side of the landing and stared down into the gray-green water. She gave a deep sigh, calmer now.

It was to be expected. She had been Cinderella. She had gone from the isolation of Lawndale, straight into the arms of Ken Parker. It would have taken sterner stuff than she was made of not to have flipped completely over his good looks and rugged charm. No doubt women far more sophisticated than she fell helplessly at his feet. Presumably his blonde had, or why would she have a change of clothes in his closet?

She had been a fool to think his interest in her went any further than a pleasant evening, and perhaps a subsequent liaison when it suited him. She had imagined the rest, just as she had imagined so many other things these last few days.

A stray thought went through her mind. She looked about, remembering the first time she had seen Ken. No, not the first time, that had been in Cincinnati.

She shook her head. That had been her imagination too, hadn't it? Ken had said he'd never been there — only, it had seemed so real to her.

She had seen him here, too, stooping down as if examining something. That, too, he said was her imagination.

Was any of it real? She put her hands to her temples and pressed, as if she would squeeze the truth into her mind. But where could she begin to look?

She opened her eyes. The water looked real. Deep and dark, but real. The wood of the landing looked real, grayed with age and weather — and there, almost at her feet, where the gray surface had been chipped away, was a patch of lighter wood that looked real, too.

She went to the end of the landing, where she had first seen Ken, and stooped down. The wood was chipped and scratched, as if a boat had tied up here recently, bumping and rubbing against the planks, revealing the paler wood beneath.

Not a boat, surely. No one came to this private landing. But she had seen a boat, a ghost ship, hadn't she? Would a ghost ship have left these marks?

The pilings had been scratched as well, as if a line had been tied there.

Or, she asked herself, am I only imagining these things as well? If I tell someone about this, will they bring me down here and show me that there are no marks on the landing or the pilings?

She looked down into the dark water. It

was like a mirror in which she saw her own reflection. A fish broke the surface for a moment, and disappeared again. He shattered her image so that her outlines and features twisted into strange shapes that did not fit together. A face that was hers and yet not hers at all.

★   ★   ★

Ken stood at the door of his cottage, staring after Ellen. He did not understand her coming or her going. She had arrived blushing and radiant, like a new bride, and a minute later she was running away like a frightened deer.

He remembered telling Nielsen that she was fragile. She was that, but there was something more than that to her, some core of strength that he didn't think she had yet discovered in herself.

She might need it before long. He had an impression that Ellen Miles had gotten into something over her head, without even knowing she had done so.

Thinking of Nielsen reminded him, he ought to call his chief. He'd been putting it off, hoping for some miracle. Nielsen would have to be told that Maggie hadn't come back from searching the Miles house. He had spent the past hour on the telephone, calling places she might have been, hoping for some freak accident that would explain why she wasn't here, and her dress was.

He'd found where she ate dinner, at her usual restaurant. She had been there early, had left in plenty of time. She had been wearing a blue silk dress. It was obvious she had come back here to change. There, the trail came to an abrupt end. Her convertible was still parked down the street.

He dialed the special number, to be used only if there was trouble. A man's voice answered guardedly, 'Hello.'

'This is Mr. Parker. I'd like to make an appointment,' Ken said.

'What time?'

'The sooner the better. Have you got one o'clock open?'

There was a pause. 'Better make it one thirty.'

'Fine. I'll be there.' Ken hung up.

★ ★ ★

Nielsen was at the waterfront when Ken arrived. Nielsen strolled idly, and paused at a story window to examine a display of boating equipment. Ken came to stand alongside him. In the glass, they could see anyone approach. They talked without looking directly at one another, but Niel's reflection watched Ken's steadily.

'Shaffer didn't come back,' Ken said. He explained about the warnings he'd tried to give her the night before, about the dress at the cottage, and the convertible. Nielsen's face remained impassive.

'Have you checked out her apartment?'

'No. I wanted to let you know the situation first. And I don't think it's likely she's there.'

'I doubt it too. Better check anyway. See that you remove anything that would link her to us.'

Ken did not respond for a moment. Nielsen was saying he didn't expect to see Maggie again. Ken didn't either, but he had not put it into such concrete thought until now.

'And?' he asked aloud.

'That's all. We sit tight.' He saw that Parker was angry. 'We can't go over there and knock on the door and ask if they happened to find a young lady of ours who is missing. Look, go check out her apartment. Let me know if she's there.' His voice and the look on his face said plainly enough he didn't think she would be.

'See ya,' he said, and drifted away. Ken was left alone at the window, studying a coil of heavy rope.

Maggie's apartment was across town, in a new complex of apartments, very chic, and exactly the sort of place one would expect a woman who looked like Maggie to live.

He went in through the service entrance. There was no answer when he rang the bell at her apartment, but he heard a sniffing inside and a low whine. The dogs were curious, on alert, but they were trained not to bark at the doorbell.

He selected a key from his ring and opened the door, cautiously calling the dogs by name before he pushed the door wide.

'Angel, Jenny, how you doing, girls?' Both dogs knew him and were obviously glad to see him. They jumped up at him as he came in, trying to lick his face.

'Maggie,' he called, closing the door. There was no answer. With the dogs trotting alongside him, trying to tell him several things with their eyes, he went through the apartment. Maggie wasn't there. He hadn't expected her to be, but he had not quite wanted to face that fact, either.

The dogs wanted to go out. He got their lead and took them down the back stairs. It was calling more attention to himself than he should have done, but what the hell, the animals couldn't manage some things by themselves. He turned them loose to run in the green space behind the complex. They came back quickly, looking relieved but unhappy. They were wondering, too, where Maggie was.

'I wish I could tell you,' he said, leading them back inside. They sniffed the ground as they went, searching for any clue.

Back in the apartment he opened a couple of cans of food and put it down for them. They attacked it gratefully, tails swinging while they ate.

He went through the apartment again, this time following Nielsen's instructions to see that nothing here would link her to them. He thought that unlikely; Maggie was too careful. About most things, at least, although obviously she hadn't been careful enough last night. In this work, it only took one slip-up. Sometimes not even that. Sometimes no matter how careful you were, things went wrong. It rarely happened twice. The first time was usually fatal.

What the apartment showed him was evidence of a lovely, charming woman. He had known her for a year or so. They had not been lovers, though they had often worked to give that impression. But they had been good friends. She had been good company as well as a good co-worker.

A photograph of her at home stood in an ebony frame atop her dresser. He had been there with her once. It was a poor farm, but it had been a pleasant place, clean and warm and filled with a 'good' atmosphere.

Her parents were in the photograph with her. He'd liked them when he met them — honest, hardworking, God-fearing — uneducated but not stupid.

He left the photograph on the dresser and looked through her other personal effects, finding nothing of significance. The nightstand had an alarm, the reading glasses she was too vain to let anyone know she needed, a box of Kleenex, and a Bible.

He opened the book, and read the inscription on the flyleaf: 'Stranger, be good to my little girl, for her mother's sake.'

He threw the book hard against the wall. The dogs jumped to attention, watching him with wide eyes.

After a minute, he went over to the book and picked it up, smoothing out a rumpled page. He put it back where he had found it, patted the dogs, and let himself out of the apartment.

★   ★   ★

Ellen heard Dawson step onto the wooden planks and turned toward him.

'Hello,' she said, forcing a smile.

'You look glum.'

'Do I?' She did not trust Dawson, even if she thought that was unfair.

'What were you looking at just now?'

'At the wood. It looks like a boat has been tied up here recently.'

'Does it?' He knelt and examined the wood at the landing's edge. 'I don't see anything except some marks that might have been made months ago, by anything. This wood is so rotten it flakes away if you even walk on it. You really ought not to be here. It isn't all that safe.'

She met his gaze evenly. 'Those marks look new to me.'

He smiled as if he did not take her altogether seriously. 'And you're an authority on boating matters?'

She weakened under his wilting look. 'Not really. But they do look like they've been made recently.'

'You're imagining things again.'

'What do you mean by that?' she asked stiffly.

'Just that. Someone's got to be frank. This isn't the first time you've imagined something that simply wasn't true. Don't you see how it's beginning to look?'

She felt a cold chill. 'Have you . . . has my aunt said anything?'

'Of course she has. She's worrying herself sick over you. I don't mean to upset you, but these little fantasies of yours are making her wonder if you're really all right. Not that she cares for herself, mind you; it's your welfare she's worried about.'

Ellen felt tears sting her eyes. She could not bear to think that her aunt might be frightened of her. 'What am I going to do?'

Dawson put an arm around her. 'Now, now,' he said gently, 'I didn't mean to make you cry. I only wanted you to face the truth. No one really believes you're ill. I think you're just lonely and unhappy, and your subconscious mind invents these little stories for you. But you know they're only fantasies, don't you?'

She nodded, although in fact she wasn't at all sure.

'You thought you saw a boat here,' he said. 'There wasn't one. I expect it was just a tree. But your mind imagined it to be a boat. And when I told you there hadn't been any boat, you came down here to look, and you've decided those old scratches on the wood prove there was a boat after all. You started with something that never existed and you've invented imaginary proofs to make it real.'

She let herself lean against him and cry, because she was unhappy and he was there, comforting her. All she could think of was that Aunt Minna had been kind, and she had made her aunt unhappy.

'You must make me a promise.'

'What is that?' The crying bout was passing. She was once again aware of things. She was uncomfortably aware of his arms about her, of the assumption of intimacy between them.

'You won't talk of these things in the future. Promise me you'll come to me with anything out of the ordinary and discuss it with me instead of your aunt or some outsider. I promise I won't laugh at you. Will you do that?'

'Yes,' she said quickly, because she wanted to escape from him. She pulled gently away from his embrace, and pushed back a strand of hair that had fallen loose. 'I am a fright. I think I should get back before anyone sees me.'

He held her hand briefly. 'Now remember, not a word of these imaginary boats and voices in the night.'

'I'll remember.' She went quickly away from him, up the path. She was still trembling, although the tears had ended. Something about the entire conversation with Dawson struck her as false.

★   ★   ★

Ellen stayed in her room throughout most of the rest of the day. Having encountered her aunt in the hall, she had found herself constrained in her aunt's company. She could not help feeling like Aunt Minna was looking sideways at her.

Despite her distrust of him, Dawson's remarks had made her feel she was suspect, as if at any minute the irons might be clapped on her wrists. She had an urge to walk on tiptoe and speak in whispers.

She would have liked to stay in the safety of her room, shutting herself off from the rest of the household; but to do so, to make a recluse of herself, would be even more significant. So she came down to dinner and made an effort to contribute to the conversation.

She did not, however, feel up to an entire evening with Dawson and Aunt Minna. When dinner was over, she excused herself, saying she thought she would go to her room.

'You've spent the entire day there,' Minna said, studying her critically. 'Aren't you feeling well?'

'To tell the truth, I'm not, entirely.'

She was spared the necessity of explaining further. Dawson said, 'I shouldn't wonder, staying out all night. You're probably just tired.'

Minna chuckled, seemingly satisfied with that answer. 'But it was fun, and that's what counts,' she said. Her expression suddenly turned serious. 'That young man didn't try anything he shouldn't have, did he?'

'No, Aunt Minna, he was a perfect gentleman. You'll excuse me?'

She was almost to the stairs when the doorbell rang. She knew Bertha and Bondage were either gone or getting ready to go, so she went herself to answer the door.

It was a shock to recognize the man standing outside. She had seen his face only once before, and briefly, but it was etched into her memory. This was the face she had seen at the French doors, the evening Dawson and Minna had been out.

He looked as startled as she. After a moment, he asked, 'Is Señor Dawson in?'

'Yes.' Her throat felt dry. This man was real. He was no ghost. Then she had seen him before, at the window, and that too had been real.

Dawson and her aunt were in conversation when she came back into the dining room.

'A man to see Dawson,' Ellen said.

'Who is he?' Dawson asked sharply.

'He didn't say. He has an accent.'

Dawson got up quickly and went into the hall. Ellen remained in the dining room. She heard their voices, but low so that their words were indistinguishable, but it sounded as if they were quarreling.

She distinctly heard Dawson say, 'In here.' A door closed loudly.

Ellen realized now that her aunt had been listening too, her head cocked to one side like a bird's. Now she sighed and looked at her niece.

'What's wrong?' she asked. 'You look as if you've seen a ghost.'

Ellen sat back down in her chair. 'I think I have. I . . . I've seen that man before.'

'In Heaven's name, where?'

'Here, looking in at the windows.'

'What on earth do you mean?'

'The night you and Dawson were out. I saw a man looking in at the French doors. It was this same man.'

'But, why didn't you mention this then?'

'I was afraid . . . I thought you would think I was mad.'

'I see.' Minna sat back in her chair, regarding her niece. She seemed to be turning something over in her mind, trying to reach a decision.

'I shall speak to Dawson. Wait here.'

Ellen waited. She heard the den door open and close, and the low murmur of voices beyond it. After a few minutes, Aunt Minna and Dawson came back together.

'Now,' Dawson said, sounding impatient and ill-tempered, 'what is this Minna tells me about this man creeping around the house and scaring you?'

'I saw him.' Ellen spoke slowly and distinctly. She wanted no one to think she was hysterical.

'When? Where?'

She told him. Dawson listened without comment, his face showing nothing of what he thought.

'Very well,' he said when she had finished, 'I shall soon get to the bottom of this.' He went out again.

Ellen and Minna waited, neither speaking nor even looking at the other. Ellen was afraid to look at her aunt, afraid that if she saw doubt there, she would begin to doubt herself.

It seemed hours, though it could only have been minutes, before Dawson came back. He wore a somber expression. Ellen knew from the first glimpse, from the set of his shoulders, from the way he avoided her eyes — she knew what he was going to say.

'You've made a mistake,' he said flatly.

Ellen stood, something close to panic rising within her. 'I didn't. He was here. I saw him.'

Dawson sighed. 'He wasn't here. The man is from South America. He showed me his passport. He just arrived in the country today.'

Ellen wanted to say that was a lie, to insist that she had seen the man, but how could she in the face of what Dawson had said?

He looked at her as if he were gravely disappointed. 'I thought you were going to tell me these things in the future, and not upset your aunt with them?'

'But, I . . . ' She bit her lip, as if to seal her thoughts inside herself.

He gave a sad shake of his head and, throwing a glance in Minna's direction, left the room again.

Ellen turned to her aunt. 'Aunt Minna,' she said, a desperate note in her voice, 'do you think I'm imagining all these things? Do you think I'm having hallucinations?'

Her aunt looked miserably unhappy. She avoided Ellen's eyes. 'I think Dawson is right, that you should not talk about these things. Perhaps you ought to go up to bed, dear. You said you weren't feeling well?'

It was a dismissal. Ellen said, 'Good night,' and started again for her room.

She felt there was more that Minna had on her mind, that she hadn't said. She was afraid to tell the truth, Ellen thought. She thinks I'm mad.

9

In her room, Ellen undressed and went to bed, but she did not sleep at once. She lay staring through the darkness at the ceiling. Some time later, there was a rap at her door. She did not reply.

The door opened. There was no word and after a pause, the door closed again. Whoever it had been had apparently decided she was asleep and had gone away.

She did fall asleep then. The house was still when she woke. The bedclothes were badly twisted and her head ached. The room felt close. She got out of bed and went to the window, throwing it open, taking deep breaths of the night air.

She heard voices, muffled voices. She shivered. Not again. Surely she was only imagining them — but they sounded real.

What if they were? If there really were people outside, it would prove that the other times might not have been delusions either. It would prove that perhaps she wasn't mad.

She leaned out the window. There was someone on the path below, the path leading through the trees. She was sure of it, sure she saw the dim outline of a man moving through the darkness.

She left the window and stole across the room as silently as she could move, to the door. It was unlocked. Not everything was the same as before.

She hesitated. If her aunt found her again wandering about the house, surely she would send her back to Lawndale.

But did that matter? As things stood, she was practically on her way there now. The only way in which she could resolve the matter was to prove she wasn't imagining things. If someone were really there, she would know she was not insane. And if she found no one . . . she did not pursue that thought.

She found her slippers by the bed and donned a robe. The house was dark. She had no flashlight and didn't know where to find one. Nor did she want to risk turning on lights. So she had to move slowly and carefully in the dark, her only light the moonlight that came through the windows.

It was easier once she reached the ground floor. She hurried to the rear of the house and let herself out the back door. It creaked when she swung it open and she froze for a moment. If someone were out there . . . ?

But if they were, it could hardly be innocent, could it? She closed the door quietly after herself and, hurrying across the terrace, stepped into the darkness of the woods. Nothing moved on the path and the only sound was the sighing of the wind in the trees.

The path led downhill, steeply in places. She had to move with caution. It was too dark to see where she stepped and there were numerous ruts and spreading tree roots. The last thing she wanted was to turn an ankle and have to lie here until morning, waiting for someone to discover her.

The air was heavy with the scent of magnolia and jasmine. The rustling of the trees lent an ominous quality.

She emerged from the trees into the little clearing where the paths separated, and paused, listening. Was that someone moving in the brush, or only the wind again? She suddenly felt all goose-pimply. Maybe she had been too rash in coming out like this. Her robe was a light one and the night air was cool.

She took a few steps toward the spot where the path continued again, and as she did so, something moved behind her. No trick of the wind, this, but the footstep of a man in the brush, and the cracking of a twig, like a rifle shot.

She turned, startled out of her wits. She saw only the dim figure of a man, a shadow separating itself from the other shadows, moving swiftly toward her.

She tried to scream, but there was no time. In only a fraction of a second she had heard him, whirled about, and had the slightest glimpse of him — then she was in his arms, seized in a violent grip, and a hand was clamped hard over her mouth.

The arms that held her were strong.

She fought against him, trying to free herself, but to no avail. Nor could she cry out with his hand clamped over her mouth.

She kicked his leg. In her soft-soled slippers, she couldn't do much harm, but she managed to make him inhale sharply.

He turned her head, burying her face hard against his jacket. He smelled damp and sweaty and . . . and male. She could not see, but she thought she heard movement, and a low murmur of voices. Then she was being half-led, half-dragged into the brush, her heart thudding.

'Be still, for God's sake.' She recognized the voice and stiffened, stunned into immobility. His grip was hurting her but she could neither break it nor ask him to lessen it. She could only stand still and wait. Again, she thought she heard something, but it was muffled, partly by the arm with which he held her close to him.

After a moment he let her go with one hand, keeping an arm about her shoulders, but loosely.

She pulled her head back, gratefully

gasping the cool night air, although she had been in no danger of suffocating. Nothing, in fact, had been harmed but her pride and her wrist, where she expected she would find a bruise soon enough.

'Where were you going?' Ken Parker asked in a whisper.

'I can't see that's any of your business,' she snapped. Unconsciously she spoke in a whisper too, but her voice was shaky. 'And what right have you got grabbing me in the dark and hauling me around like a sack of potatoes?'

'You haven't said what on earth you're doing creeping around in the woods at night.'

'And you haven't said why you dragged me into the bushes like this.' They were well off the path, in the shelter of a big oak tree. No one going by on the path would have seen them here unless they knew to look in this direction.

'I thought you might scream.'

'I certainly would have.' She rubbed her wrist.

'And you'd have roused the whole

neighborhood,' he said in a matter-of-fact voice, as if this explained everything away. 'I can't think what your aunt would have thought, you and I out here together in the woods, you in your robe and screaming like a banshee. I thought it most discreet to keep you quiet until you were a little calmer.'

'How thoughtful of you,' she said sharply. 'You scared me half out of my wits in the process, of course, and managed to keep me from seeing whatever it was you were up to.'

He laughed. It seemed so genuine that it managed to take a little, but not all, of the wind out of her sails.

'I was out for some air. I thought I heard someone down by the river, so I started along to investigate. This isn't the best part of town any more, I suppose you've noticed. I paused here, by the clearing, and then you came along. To tell you the truth, you gave me a hell of a scare. I reacted without thinking.'

'Reacted rather violently, if you ask me. Why did you drag me in here, off the path?'

'I thought I heard someone coming up from the landing. There was some trouble a while back, some local toughs. I thought discretion would be the better part of valor. And I couldn't exactly explain it all to you just then, could I?'

He smiled. He looked perfectly relaxed, perfectly normal, as if nothing important had happened. 'Now, your turn. What were you doing out here?'

She said, a little sullenly because she wasn't feeling kindly toward him just then, 'I thought I heard someone too. I came out to take a look.'

'Kind of dangerous, don't you think?' He cocked an eyebrow. 'A woman, alone, in the dark.'

'As it turns out, the only danger I was in was from you. Who *was* out here, by the way, besides us, I mean?'

He shook his head. 'Apparently no one. I thought I heard someone coming up the path, but if it was, they heard us and got scared and highballed it some other way. I didn't see a soul.'

'Someone went by while we were wrestling.'

He gave his head another shake. 'Not a soul.'

She looked steadily at him for a moment. The moonlight was enough to make out his face, but she could not read its expression.

'You too,' she murmured and went to step past him.

He grabbed her wrist again. 'What was that supposed to mean?'

'You're hurting my wrist.'

He let it go at once but he had stepped in front of her, blocking her way, and for the moment he had abandoned his pretense of nonchalance, in which she hadn't believed anyway. He looked tense and alert, dangerous, and she found herself frightened all over again. Something had changed, suddenly, but she didn't know what, or why.

'What did you mean by that?' he asked again. 'You too.'

'Only that everyone is convinced that I'm imagining things. I keep hearing things and seeing things, and everyone keeps insisting that there's nothing there. That's why I came out tonight, if you want to know. Because this isn't the first time I've thought I heard someone here, and when I mention it to Aunt Minna or Dawson Elliot, they tell me I'm having dreams. But what they really mean is, I'm losing my mind. So I wanted to see for myself if it was real, if there was someone here. And I found you. And now you too want me to believe that what I heard was only my imagination. But I don't believe that. And there are only two possibilities. Either I'm right and everybody — including Dawson and you and my aunt, who has been so kind to me — everybody is lying to me. Or I'm wrong, and I am imagining things, and . . . '

It caught up with her all at once, the fear that her mind was slipping, the anger on being treated like a piece of baggage. It hit her so unexpectedly that she was no more prepared for what happened next than he was. She began to cry.

To her further surprise, he reacted with surprising tenderness to her tears. He put his arm about her again and pulled her once more against him, but this time in a comforting way that was altogether tender and gentle.

'And you think it means you should be back in that hospital?'

She blubbered a not very distinct 'yes' against his cheek, and moved her head up and down.

'All right,' he said, putting a finger under her chin and tilting her face so that she was looking at him again, 'I'm sorry. I didn't know about the rest of it or I wouldn't have tried so clumsily to lie to you. You weren't imagining anything. There really was someone here tonight on the path from the landing. That's why I dragged you in there. I really was afraid for you. And I lied because I thought it would worry you if you knew you had strangers prowling around out here from time to time.'

She sniffled. 'Who were they?'

'I don't know. I was too busy trying to keep you still. Now, tell me about the other times, and we'll see if we can put your mind to rest there too.'

'There's nothing to tell. Just that I've

thought I heard things before.'

'When?' His interest was too keen to be casual.

She shook her head. 'I don't know which nights. A few nights ago. And a few nights before that. I'd better go in.'

'Lord, yes, you must be frozen, dressed like that. Come on, I'll walk you back up to the house.'

'It isn't necessary.'

'It is to me.'

He took her arm. She saw, as they began to move toward the house, that he hadn't a flashlight either. She knew why she didn't have one, but he didn't have the same excuse. So why was he risking a broken ankle on these paths, unless he simply didn't want someone to see him?

They walked silently. He seemed satisfied that he had answered her questions and she was too confused to talk intelligently.

He stopped at the edge of the terrace. 'I hadn't better come any closer,' he said. 'If anyone should happen to look out and see us together like this, it would cause quite a stir, don't you think?'

She managed a wan smile. 'Probably no more than my being out alone. I'm rather suspect, don't you see?'

He looked down into her face for a moment. She had an impression he was searching it for something. 'Poor kid,' he said.

Then he kissed her, so suddenly that she was far too surprised even to respond. And by the time she had awakened to the feel of his lips on hers and realize how nice it felt, the kiss was ended and he was gone, disappearing into the darkness of the trees, leaving her to stand alone on the terrace, shivering.

★   ★   ★

In a way, she had exchanged one concern for another. It had been a relief in a sense to see Ken Parker in the woods. She knew for certain she had not been imagining people there. And though she thought he had lied to her, he had at least not tried to make her think she was having hallucinations. So he had given her a little confidence in herself.

The question now was, what did she do with her new evidence that she was not losing her mind?

Ken had lied to her about why he was there and about who else had been there. Why the lies, and what was the real reason he was there, skulking about in the night? She had seen him doing so before, and she was sure now that had been real too.

He had lied when she had first seen him on the boat landing, too. He had been looking for something then, and had denied it.

All she had needed, however, was confirmation that part of the things she had seen were true, and she was ready now to believe that it had all been true. She did not know how all the pieces fit together, but she did know the pieces were real, and that properly put together they would form a picture.

The problem for her was that if she told Aunt Minna and Dawson about seeing Ken, while it would settle some of the questions in their minds regarding her, it would also raise questions regarding Ken — the same questions she had been asking herself.

That was surely inviting trouble for Ken. Of course, it might very well be that he deserved it. Whatever her feelings for him might be, it certainly appeared he was up to some sort of skullduggery. It was one thing, however, to think that someone you cared for might be doing something wrong, and quite another thing to point an accusing finger.

She threw back the covers and got out of bed, stretching on tiptoe. She felt greatly changed this morning. Today the world was solid, if troubled.

Minna and Dawson were in the breakfast room when she came down. Mrs. Bondage was just clearing away Dawson's plates.

'Good morning, dear,' Minna greeted her. 'Bondage, bring Ellen's breakfast.'

Ellen greeted them both. She thought that her aunt was distant this morning. A day ago, that observation would have sent her into a panic, but now she not only understood the reason but knew that she could somehow cope with it.

Bondage brought her a cup of coffee. Dawson's newspaper was lying on the table where he had put it aside after reading it. Ellen's eyes fell on the front page and the hand lifting the cup to her mouth shook so that she spilled her coffee.

'Are you all right?' Aunt Minna asked.

'Yes, of course. May I see that?' she asked of Dawson, picking up his newspaper without waiting for a reply.

The front page featured a large picture of a woman, a lovely blonde woman. According to the headlines, she had been found dead. Foul play was suspected.

Ellen stared at the photograph, looking deep into eyes that had only a short time before sparkled gaily. She had only seen the woman once, and then briefly, but she had made an indelible impression. In her mind, Ellen saw her in her elegant tweeds, with her majestic dogs and her big, expensive convertible. There was no doubt in her mind — this was the same woman she had seen with Ken.

Her eyes quickly scanned the story

accompanying the picture. The woman had been identified as Maggie Shaffer. Her body had been washed ashore on a nearby beach. It looked as if she had drowned, but the police suspected that was not the case. Preliminary evidence suggested she had been dead when she entered the water. An autopsy was scheduled.

In other words, Ellen thought, reading between the lines, she had been murdered. The word was like an electric shock in her mind. Shock that such a breathtakingly lovely creature should have come to so abrupt and ugly an end.

That alone would have been enough to unnerve her, but another thought was buzzing persistently around in her mind. Had Ken anything to do with this? He knew Maggie Shaffer, certainly. According to the newspaper story, the woman had apparently died the night before last — the night she and Minna and Ken had gone to the opera.

Of course, Ken had been with them for most of the night — but she could not forget the worry she had seen in his eyes throughout that evening, the distraction that had made him seem as if he were not with them at all, or the numerous phone calls.

Something major had been on his mind through the dinner and the opera — something, unless she were mistaken, to do with this woman, Maggie. Whatever-it-was had been resolved somewhere in the course of the evening, so that later he was able to relax completely with her and show her one of the most exciting nights of her life.

The evidence against him was damning: his otherwise strange behavior, the creeping around at night, his hiding the truth, his surreptitious manner.

She suddenly became aware that her aunt had said something to her. She had been staring all this while fixedly at the newspaper. She looked up from it to find both Dawson and her aunt regarding her. Dawson looked strained. Minna was puzzled and worried.

'What is it?' Minna asked. 'You look as if you've seen a ghost.'

'Perhaps I have. Excuse me, please.'

Ellen put her coffee aside and got up so suddenly that she nearly knocked over Mrs. Bondage, who was coming in just then with a tray of bacon and eggs. Ellen dashed around her.

'But, your breakfast,' Minna cried.

'Not hungry,' Ellen replied. She left them all staring after her and fairly ran from the house. She had brought the newspaper with her, clutching it tightly. She ran along the path through the trees, across the clearing, and up the path that led to Ken's cottage.

She wasted no time on pleasantries. He had no more than opened the door when she shoved the newspaper at him and demanded, 'Do you know anything about this?'

He was startled by the directness of her question. He studied the picture for a moment, not so much as if he were trying to recognize it, but more, she thought, as if he were trying to select the right words for an answer.

He looked up at her. His blue eyes were filled with pain. 'Why do you ask?'

'Because I have to know. You do know

her, don't you? It is the woman I saw with you, isn't it?'

He handed the paper back to her. 'Don't ask me about these things, please.'

'But why?'

'Because I don't want to have to tell you again that you're imagining things.'

'You mean, when I'm really not?'

He took her hand in an impetuous gesture. 'Please,' he said in a low, intense voice, 'trust me. If I have to answer your questions now, I'll have to lie to you, and I don't want to do that.'

They stood in silence for several seconds, looking at one another. Finally he let go of her hand. He looked incredibly tired. More than that, even — beaten down.

She said nothing more. She turned and left him standing in the open door. She could not answer him because she could not refuse what he asked, and yet she could not give him a promise she had no right to keep.

He knew something about poor Maggie Shaffer's death. He had as much as confessed that. Something he could not tell her, which certainly must mean something not very nice.

Her heart told her to trust him, as he had asked. He had asked her not to demand answers to her questions and she had granted him that request. But the questions remained, with their awful implications.

It was not only the two of them who were involved, either. He was up to something that surely involved Aunt Minna's house and the landing. Even if it were nothing serious, it would seem that her aunt had a right to know of this.

It had become very serious indeed, however, if a murder, or even a suspected murder, were involved — a murder in which she was sure Ken had some part, however indirect.

It did not matter what her heart told her, or how much she wanted to be on his side and help him. She could not stand by and see her aunt in any way endangered, or dragged into some sort of scandal.

She had to tell her aunt everything, and pray that in doing so, she was not betraying Ken.

Dawson and her aunt were still in the breakfast room. She heard them talking as she approached, but when she came in they fell silent, both of them looking hard at her.

'Ellen,' Minna said in her most commanding tone of voice, 'I want an explanation for your behavior. You ran out of here as if you had been shot from a cannon.'

'It was this.' Ellen handed her the newspaper.

Dawson said sharply, 'That woman who drowned?'

'The police don't think she drowned.'

'And I hope you don't know anything about it,' he said.

'I knew her. That is, I saw her recently.'

Dawson made an impatient gesture. 'Oh, not another face at a window — '

'No, I didn't imagine it.' She spoke directly to her aunt. 'I did see her, and so did you, Aunt. She was with Mr. Parker recently, on the terrace. They were walking together. She had two dogs on leashes. She got into a red convertible and drove away, and he came down to where you and I were standing and asked if I wanted to see the park. You must remember.' She said all this in a rush of words, before either of them could interrupt her and try again to tell her she was imagining things. This was real, she knew it was real.

Aunt Minna gave her a surprised look. She had detected an unfamiliar note in her niece's voice, something she hadn't heard before, and it so caught her attention that she searched Ellen's face for a moment, wondering.

Dawson had taken a deep breath as Ellen was speaking. Now he asked, 'What has Parker got to do with this? Was he connected with this woman in some way?'

'He was a friend of hers. Oh, Aunt Minna, you do remember that day? You can't think I just imagined it.'

Minna nodded. 'Yes, I remember it quite well. And I remember he was with a young woman. I can't say that her face remained in my mind, because there was no reason for me to pay any particular attention to her. But certainly it could be the same young woman.'

'She is the same.'

Minna smiled faintly. She'd always said her niece had pluck. If there was anything she couldn't stand, it was someone who backed down too easily. 'All right,' she said, 'I believe you, if you say that she is.' She saw that Ellen wasn't entirely convinced. 'I really do believe you,' she emphasized.

Ellen gave a deep sigh of relief. She pulled out her chair and sat. 'I didn't imagine it. And I didn't imagine any of the rest, either . . . the people in the woods at night, the — '

Dawson interrupted her in a voice of annoyance. 'Oh, for Heaven's sake, we aren't going all through that again, are we?'

'But it's true,' Ellen said firmly. 'All of it. May I have some coffee, please, and I'll tell you everything. Everything I know, that is.'

Bondage came to pour coffee and Ellen had to assure her she did not want more eggs, and that this was no reflection on the breakfasts she had been served in the past, but she was simply not hungry this morning.

When they were settled with coffee and Bondage had returned to the kitchen, Ellen began her explanations.

'I know,' she said, 'that you've both thought that I have imagined some of the things I've mentioned to you. I know you thought I was mentally unbalanced.' Minna started to say something but Ellen silenced her with a gesture. 'I'm not blaming you. I can see how it looked. I began to believe that myself. But I was mistaken, and so were you.

'Last night again I thought I heard someone outside. I went out to investigate and I found Mr. Parker in the woods.'

Dawson's eyes went wide and he leaned forward in his chair. 'Parker? You saw him out there?'

'Yes, and he wasn't the only one either.'

Minna and Dawson exchanged glances. 'Who else did you see?' Minna asked.

'Or think you saw?' Dawson added.

Ellen had no mind to be intimidated that way, however. 'I didn't see anyone else,' she said, 'but I heard other people.'

'You had no business out there like that,' Dawson said. His face had gone ashen. Ellen could see at least that the two of them were taking her story quite seriously. No one was scoffing now.

'I had to prove to myself that I wasn't losing my mind. I had lost all confidence in what my senses told me. Much more of that and I might very well have gone off the deep end.'

To her surprise, Minna laughed. 'We've been fools,' she said to Dawson. More soberly, she said to Ellen, 'Of course you weren't losing your mind.'

'Never mind that,' Dawson snapped. 'I want to know why Parker was out there at all.'

Ellen explained briefly about her encounter with Ken and his explanation for why he was there. She did not supply all the details. There was no reason they needed know that she had cried, or that he had kissed her.

'I don't know what all this means,' she concluded. 'I don't know if there is any connection between Ken's watching this house and the death of that poor girl. But he is watching the house, and I thought you ought to know.'

A lengthy silence followed. Dawson scowled thoughtfully and scratched his chin. Minna regarded her niece. 'Are you emotionally involved with this Mr. Parker?'

'That's of no consequence,' Ellen said.

Dawson ignored this exchange, lost in his own thoughts. After a moment, he said, 'We've got to know who this Parker really is and what his business is here. But how are we going to find out?'

'You could ask him,' Ellen said.

'And get the same evasive answers he gave you. No, that's no good.' He looked across the table at her. 'But you could find out?'

'Me? Good Heavens, how?'

'Talk to him. Butter him up. Or, better yet, you could search that cottage of his.'

'I couldn't. I wouldn't know how to get in, or what to look for.'

'I have a key,' Minna said quietly. 'The Creightons gave it to me ages ago. They were expecting something delivered and asked me if I would take delivery and have it put in the cottage. They never did ask for the key back, and I never thought to give it to them.'

'That's perfect, then,' Dawson said.

'But it's nonsense,' Ellen said. 'If you think his place ought to be searched, why don't you go?'

'Because if he saw me hanging around, he would certainly get suspicious. But he isn't likely to think anything's afoot if he sees you.'

'There's some sense to that,' Minna agreed. She did not seem altogether happy with the direction of the conversation, however.

Ellen turned to her. 'Aunt, do you really think I should do this?'

'I would certainly like to know who he is and what his interest is in me,' Minna said.

'Wouldn't it be simpler just to call the police,' Ellen said, 'and put all this to them?'

'Indeed it would be,' Dawson said. 'But consider things from Mr. Parker's point of view. We may be getting him into a lot of trouble for nothing. If it turned out his interest was entirely innocent, say he wanted to use the house in some book of his, why then, the whole affair could be forgotten.

'But if there's any indication that he's up to no good, then it would be the time to go to the police. It's to his benefit for us to investigate a little further on our own before we do anything drastic. Of course, if you'd rather we bring the police in at once, regardless of what trouble we may be causing for him, why . . . ' He shrugged to show it was of no great consequence to him either way.

'No,' Ellen said with a sigh. 'I'd rather try to resolve it ourselves, if we could. I'll do as you suggest, but I have to say, it goes against the grain.'

Minna patted her hand. 'I will be grateful if you do this. And Dawson is right, it will be easier for you than for either of us.'

Ellen could see that they were right, so far as it went. And having brought all this into the open, she felt she had an obligation to see it through.

Something in her recoiled, however, at

the thought of spying on Ken. She did not know quite why this should be so, since he so obviously had been spying on them.

She did not admit, even to herself, that she was a little afraid of what she might learn.

10

Ken parked his car on the street. It was evening. His mind was preoccupied with the meeting he had just left. Nielsen was unhappy, and with good reason. Things were going pretty badly. Everyone had been shocked by Maggie's death, no one worse than he.

Then there was Ellen Miles, with those doe-like eyes. He couldn't understand why he was letting her get under his skin. He had worked on assignments involving women before. He had always considered himself immune to anything more than an elementary physical reaction or, at most, the sort of comradeship he'd had with Maggie.

Nielsen thought he was behaving like a fool, and when you came right down to it, Nielsen was probably right. He should have done as Nielsen suggested originally and used Ellen to get into the house, if only through her mind and eyes. Even assuming she was entirely innocent, and he was convinced by now she was, he would not necessarily be doing her any harm that way. He had experience. He knew how to let a woman down gently when the job was finished, so she suffered nothing more than a slightly bruised ego, and sometimes not even that. It was standard operating procedure.

There was some risk, of course. Sometimes a woman simply got too involved, let her emotions get out of hand. Then you just had to break if off, hard and quick, and trust her to get over it.

So what was it that scared him about Ellen Miles? The fact that she looked like she would get too involved emotionally? Yes, he was sure she was the type.

Which meant she would get hurt eventually, if he tried to use her. She was vulnerable, and doubly so because of her recent history. A shock now to her emotional balance . . . and she wasn't the sort to 'get over' things quickly.

All right, he was afraid she would get hurt. Damn it, Maggie had gotten hurt. It was part of the game. It happened, and that was no reason to drag his feet the way he was doing. Someone always got hurt and you had to balance that against what you were seeking to accomplish. The end, if it was big enough and right enough, did justify the means.

A narrow path and a flight of rough stone steps led about and behind the Creighton's main house, down to the cottage. He had reached the bottom of the steps before he saw the rectangle of light thrown by the window across the flagstone terrace.

Someone was inside the cottage.

He remembered he had left his notes in his computer, and the computer running, and cursed himself for a fool. He ought at least to have shut the computer down, password protected, which would keep any casual snooper at bay. He had been careless, and in his work that could lead to unenviable results.

He slipped his hand inside his jacket and brought out a small revolver, picturing the interior of the cottage. No place for anyone to hide, except behind the door. And they wouldn't be expecting him or they wouldn't have left the light on.

Unless it was a trap. In that case, he'd have to do some very fast shooting and hope the trap wasn't set too well.

The lock was the old-fashioned kind that needed a key. He had his own key in his pocket. Whoever was inside had come with another — it was still in the lock. That meant the door was unlocked. Good. He could get it open fast, with no fumbling and no tell-tale grating of the key in the lock to announce his arrival.

He crept to the door, gun in hand. He had already clicked the safety off. His finger, on the trigger, was ready.

He paused, took a deep breath, and put his hand to the knob. In one quick motion, he turned it and threw the door open, slamming it back hard against the wall in case anyone was hiding there.

He had the gun leveled straight before him. As the door crashed open, someone moved inside, coming across the room toward him. Instinctively his finger tightened on the trigger.

She had waited until sunset, although from an upstairs window she had seen Ken's car drive away from the terrace late in the afternoon. Somehow she felt she wanted the cover of darkness. Finally, when the sun had descended below the horizon, she set out for the yellow cottage.

The cottage windows were dark. There was no sign of life. Still, she hesitated at the door. This was where he lived. The very air about it seemed different, electrically charged with his presence. She did not want to do this, like a thief in the night.

Well, she had promised her aunt to make the effort. And whatever her feelings might be for Ken, the evidence suggested that he was up to some sort of mischief.

She put the key in the lock. It turned easily and the door swung open. She went in, clicking on a light, and looked about her.

There was not a great deal to search:

only one room with its studio couches that were both sofas and beds; the chair; the dresser; the desk, with a computer humming atop it. Through an open door at one end she could see the kitchen, and at the other end a bathroom and dressing area.

If there were anything to be found, it would probably be in the desk, or on the computer. She looked in that direction for several seconds, as if willing them to speak and tell her their secrets. They remained mute.

An open book lay face down on the table by the chair. Curious, she picked it up, quite aware that she was trying to delay the necessity of prying. The book was by C.P. Snow, which surprised her. It did not fit with the general impression she had of Ken Parker. Snow was an intellectual's writer. The book, however, looked well-thumbed, as if he had read it through more than once.

She looked again at the desk and the computer, but she could not yet make herself go to them. Instead, she sat down in the chair and looked at the page to which the book was opened.

'Anyone who had lived at all believed in luck,' she read. 'Anyone who had avoided total failure had to believe in luck. Why it was luck merely to survive . . . '

Luck seemed to her a shallow word. There was something, all right, that caused things to happen in a certain way, but she thought it went deeper than the sort of willy-nilly thing she called luck.

Whatever it was, of course, had helped her to survive a difficult time, when matters seemed to have been taken out of her hands.

Very well, then, what else did one need to survive? Wisdom? But perhaps wisdom was the least important of all the tools of survival. There would always be something beyond one's comprehension, some knowledge for which one would have to trust someone else.

In the end, perhaps trust was the answer. You had to trust someone or something, whether it was a person or a religious belief, or merely luck. Or even trust in oneself. So long as you could trust, surely you could survive.

Her thoughts came back to the present with a jolt. Trust? What a fool she was. Not trusting, she had come here to pry into Ken's private life. Odious enough in itself, but more so because he did trust her, and had asked her to trust him.

If he were involved in any sort of wrongdoing, he had certainly taken a grave chance, trusting her, in making the implied confession he had made earlier, that he did indeed know something regarding Maggie Shaffer's death, something he couldn't share with her at present.

He had not tried to convince her she was imagining things, as her aunt and Dawson had done. That was true of their meeting in the woods, too. If he were a murderer, which she could not for a moment believe, he could as easily have wrung her neck then. He had not, and when he learned the reason for her miserable confusion, he had been careful to provide an explanation, even if a not-quite-honest one, that did not hinge upon her being mentally unbalanced.

Trust. Yes, he trusted her, for whatever

reasons of his own. And because she loved him, she must trust him.

She clapped the book shut, eager to be out of here, and started for the door.

She did not reach it. It burst open, as suddenly as if before a storm.

And as suddenly, she found herself staring down the barrel of a gun.

11

Luckily, his reflexes were fast. As instantly as Ken's finger had tightened on the trigger, so did it relax without firing at her. She had frozen in the center of the room, staring at him with her frightened eyes wider than ever.

He lowered the revolver to his side. 'What on earth are you doing here?' he asked. He didn't have to pretend to be surprised. She was the last person he had expected to find.

'I was asked to search your place,' she said frankly. She had taken the plunge.

'By whom?'

'My aunt and the man who boards with her.' She could not keep from looking at the gun.

He followed her glance and in one quick movement had put it away somewhere inside his jacket. 'Dawson Elliot?' She nodded.

'Find anything?' He almost made his

voice sound amused.

'I didn't look.'

'Why not?'

'Because . . . ' She gave a quick shrug. 'It didn't seem fair.'

He relaxed a little. He closed the door and locked it, and handed that key to her.

'Yours?'

'My aunt's.'

'I'm going to have a drink,' he said over his shoulder. 'Want one?'

'Thank you, no.' She felt quite intoxicated enough.

He poured himself a lot of Scotch and took a sip. He felt unnerved, but not by finding someone in his cottage. He'd been in similar situations plenty of times, but he'd never before met a woman who could face a man with a gun and tell him she had decided against searching his quarters because it didn't seem fair — and make him believe it.

He took another drink and a deep breath, and said, 'Look, I'm going to tell you something. I'm not a writer. That's what we call a cover. I'm an agent for the United States Government.' And, he thought, if Nielsen heard me tell her that — *her* — he'd shoot me and say it was only fair.

'Why are you here? It has something to do with my aunt, hasn't it?'

'I can't tell you any more. By all rights I shouldn't have told you what I did. Let's just say I thought it was fair. Do you believe me?'

'Yes.'

'Why?'

She smiled. 'Why did you believe me when I said I hadn't searched this place? Sooner or later you have to decide who or what you're going to believe. Otherwise you really will go crazy.'

They were silent for a moment. She looked at him, a little shyly. 'If I were completely honest, I'd admit it had to do in some measure with your kissing me last night.'

He put his drink aside and crossed the space between them in three quick strides, taking her in his arms, and kissed her, not as he had so briefly that night on the terrace, but long and hard and urgently.

When their lips finally parted, they were both breathing hard, as if it had been a tremendous exertion. Her eyes were still closed.

'Look at me,' he said very softly. She opened her eyes.

He had faced dangers of a thousand varieties, but never had he felt so weak, so helpless, and at the same time so masculine and protective, as he did with her.

'I've killed men,' he said in a deliberately emotionless tone. 'I don't mean in the heat of battle, as a soldier. Once in an alley I shot a man in the back when he was trying to escape. I had to. I'd broken my foot and if I hadn't killed him, he'd have gotten away and caused thousands of deaths. But I shot him in the back without a moment's hesitation.'

'Why are you telling me this?'

'Because you've got to know what I am. If I could have prevented this somehow, I would have. I'm the last man on earth for a woman to be involved with. The last man on earth you should be involved with.'

'But I am involved. And I already know what you are.'

She felt no fear of him, nor of what she was feeling. She had a new confidence, a gift of her love. He was afraid of what was happening between them, but her heart told her to trust.

'I may hurt you.'

'Never.' She brought her lips up to his again and felt his arms tighten fiercely about her as his mouth found hers.

★ ★ ★

She said, quite irrelevantly, 'I've always envied those women with the golden tans. I'm so pale.'

He wondered how it was that she was so ignorant of her own loveliness. She did not know that the moonlight pouring over her just now had turned her pale skin to gleaming alabaster that seemed, like the moon itself, to be lighted from beneath its surface, a gleaming softness that invited the touch of a man's hand.

He raised his arm to glance at his watch. 'You'd better be getting back before your aunt starts to worry.'

'Oh, Lord, they're going to want to know what happened.'

'If I were you, I wouldn't tell them.'

She laughed and stood, flicking on a light. 'What am I going to tell them, though?'

He grew sober. 'Nothing.'

'All right,' she said simply.

He breathed a little more easily, and got up as well. 'Do you understand,' he said, 'that I just can't explain all this to you yet?'

'I understand. It's all right.' She paused, and said, 'Ken, I am fond of my aunt. I can't know what she's involved herself in — no, that's all right, I'm not asking, I know you'll tell me in good time. I only wanted to say, she's truly a good person. She wouldn't knowingly do anything bad.'

'I'll remember. Come on, I'll walk you home. I want to. Anyway, I need to ask you a few questions. Will you mind? It makes you something of an informer.'

'I don't mind, if it helps you,' she said, going out before him. 'But I don't think

I'll help much. You probably already know more than I do.'

He could not tell her, and did not know if she realized, that she herself was considered a suspect by the men he worked for, and that he not only had to learn about the goings on at her aunt's house, but had to clear her name as well.

In order to convince Nielsen of her innocence, he was probably going to have to tell him about what had just happened. He could well imagine how Nielsen would view it. At the moment he hated his superior.

They reached the edge of the terrace. He took her hand, looking troubled.

'What is it?' she asked.

He hesitated. 'I wish you were out of this.' After a moment, he said, 'They've been bringing something into the house at night, from the landing. I need to know where it's at.'

'I'll look.' She did not mind. She would have done anything he asked.

'It's dangerous.'

'But my aunt . . . '

'Dangerous,' he repeated firmly. 'Don't

take any chances. Don't even look around if there's anybody in the house. I don't want anyone getting the idea you're working for me. But if they should all be out, and you have a chance to poke around a bit . . . '

'I'll try.'

He kissed her again. Then he was gone.

Aunt Minna and Dawson were in the library when she came in. They heard her and came into the hall.

'Thank Heaven,' Minna said, putting a hand to her breast. 'I was so worried.'

'What happened?' Dawson demanded. 'You've been gone hours.'

She tried to think of them as enemies — not hers, specifically, but Ken's. It was impossible to think of her aunt that way, though. She felt sure that her aunt could not knowingly be involved in anything wicked and she trusted Ken to discover this for himself.

She could well believe ill of Dawson, but not knowing what he was supposed to be guilty of, it was hard to imagine even him as an enemy. It was tempting to simply tell them the truth and let it go at that — but she had to trust Ken, and he trusted her.

'Not quite two hours,' she said aloud. 'And nothing happened. I went to Mr. Parker's cottage thinking he was out, but he was in. I couldn't just say, 'oh, excuse me, I came over to search your place while you were out.' So I had to pretend it was a neighborly visit, and we sat and chatted for a while.'

Aunt Minna compressed her lips. 'In my day, a young lady did not pay an unchaperoned call upon a young man.'

'In this case, however, my visit was not my idea. Anyway, Mr. Parker was a perfect gentleman.' Which was true as far as it went. 'And if you'll excuse me, I am tired. I think I'll go up to my room.'

She climbed the stairs, aware that both of them continued to watch her, Dawson in a coolly appraising manner. She felt rather pleased with herself. She had never dreamed she possessed any acting talent.

12

Ellen slept that night with the memory of Ken's kiss on her lips. In the morning, however, other memories came back.

It was incredible that he should be what he said he was, or that she should be involved in such matters. It was even more bewildering that Aunt Minna should be involved in anything that would arouse the interest of the government. She could only suppose that, however Ken tried to convince her of the danger, this was not after all a very serious matter.

She would take him at his word nonetheless, and be cautious. At the earliest opportunity, she would look around the house to see if she could find anything hidden. Admittedly, that was made a bit more difficult in that she did not know what it was she was looking for. If it was something so very out of the ordinary, however, surely she would know at once when she had found it.

The opportunity to search the house presented itself to her sooner than she might have expected. Dawson went out during the afternoon with the explanation that he had some research to do on his book. Soon afterward, Minna came into the library where Ellen was reading.

'I've got to go for a dress fitting,' she said. 'Would you like to come along to get out of the house?'

'No, I think I feel like loafing. Will you be gone long?'

'As slow as that woman is, it will surely be hours.' Minna hesitated on the verge of saying something more.

'You've got something else on your mind,' Ellen said. 'You may as well out with it.'

'Bertha and Bondage had asked if they might leave a little early. Dawson said he would have dinner downtown, and I thought if you went with me, we could have a sandwich . . . '

'But you're worried about my starving if they don't stay to prepare dinner for me?' Ellen said with a laugh. 'You needn't worry about me. I can manage quite well.

As a matter of fact, I think I may order in a pizza. By all means send them away.'

'Pomfret will be with me. It will leave you all alone in the house, and with that Mr. Parker prowling about.'

'I don't think Mr. Parker will attempt to harm me. Goodness knows, he's had plenty of opportunities before now. I'll be quite all right, really.'

'Well, if you say so,' Aunt Minna said, but reluctantly. She went to dismiss the servants.

Ellen continued to read and to wait. She heard Bondage and Bertha leave. Aunt Minna stopped in the doorway to ask if Ellen was sure she'd be all right.

'Positive,' Ellen assured her.

Ellen went to the front window and waited until she saw her aunt climb into the Packard and saw it drive away from the curb. Now, she thought, was her time to scour the place. She felt a pang of guilt, searching her aunt's house, but it was offset by her conviction that her aunt was not involved in anything really bad, and by the knowledge that she was helping Ken.

It was a big house, however, with many rooms. 'I might as well make it top to bottom,' she said aloud. She went to the kitchen, where she found a flashlight, and started up the stairs to the attic.

★   ★   ★

Downtown, Dawson was in a hotel room with Captain Rivera, the man Ellen had seen at the library window. The room was cloudy with cigar smoke, and scattered around were a number of paper cups that had held coffee. They had spread several maps and charts over the surface of the bed and for several hours now they had been going over these, discussing various details, drawing lines with marking pens.

On the surface of the largest map were several cardboard cutouts of boats, and these they had moved about at intervals, grouping and regrouping them.

Finally, they stood, shaking hands.

'Till tonight, then,' Dawson said. He left the room. In the hall, he shunned the elevator, an old-fashioned one with an attendant, and took the stairs instead. He wanted to be seen by as few people as possible who might remember him later and connect him with this hotel and Captain Rivera.

The lobby was busy. No one paid him any attention as he crossed it and went out. He paused on the street. He had intended to eat dinner out, but in fact he was not very hungry. He decided instead that he would go directly home, and looked about for a taxi.

★　★　★

It was preying on Minna's mind that she ought not to have left Ellen alone in the house. It was not that she thought Ellen was in any danger, but rather that Ellen might be a danger to what she and Dawson had planned. There had been that unfortunate business when she had seen that fool, Rivera, peering in at the windows, and had later recognized him when he came to see Dawson.

The point was, there was always a risk. Tonight one of the boats was scheduled to come in. That was later, of course, but suppose through some error it came early . . .

She leaned forward to tap Pomfret on the shoulder. 'I've changed my mind,' she said. 'Take me back to the terrace.'

★ ★ ★

The attic was filled with old boxes and trunks of all sorts, but there was such a layer of dust on everything that she found it hard to believe they hadn't been there for years. She flashed the light around, trying to spy something peculiar.

The house itself is peculiar, she thought. Where else would one find a moon garden . . . ?

Of course, she thought. She was looking in the wrong place. If one were hiding something here, in this house, it would not be in the attic.

She went quickly down the stairs, straight through to the library. The hidden door behind the bookcases opened at her touch and she was in the moon garden.

The night Dawson had showed her the moon garden, he had suggested she might want to see the cellar where the slaves had once been imprisoned, and Minna had been shocked at the suggestion.

Ellen had thought then that Dawson was teasing her aunt, and now she understood why. Whatever was hidden in the house, whatever it was Ken was looking for, she was certain she would find in the cellar.

The cellar doors lay nearly horizontal. They were heavy but they opened with an ease that suggested they were used regularly. Rough stone steps led downward. Praying she would not encounter any prowling rats, she descended.

Something brushed her face and made her squeak. She slapped at it and found it was a string dangling from a light bulb in the ceiling. She pulled it and the room was illuminated with its yellow glare.

The cellar was packed full of boxes and crates, and there were no cobwebs or layers of dust to suggest they had been there for years. She shined her light around. There were dozens, scores of boxes.

The lid of one was partially askew, as if

someone had opened it to check the contents. She went to it, shining the light inside.

Guns. Guns of every conceivable sort, pistols and revolvers and rifles, all in a jumble inside the crate. She stared in bewilderment. She went among the boxes, shining her light. There were others that had been opened. She saw more guns, and ammunition. One box, still nailed shut, had the word 'dynamite' stenciled on the outside and another said 'grenades.'

The cellar was a storehouse of arms, a mini-arsenal.

Her mind reeled. For a moment she wondered if these were weapons left over from the slave-running days — but no, these boxes were too new, too dust-free, the weapons too modern.

What could it mean? Guns meant warfare of some sort, but she could think of no warfare in which her aunt could be involved. It was true, in her heart she still fought the Civil War, but Aunt Minna was not dotty enough to actually want to revive that conflict.

A sound outside startled her from her thoughts. Someone was coming. She looked around frantically, but there was no place to hide, and no time to escape. She had just turned toward the door when someone blocked the light from it, and a moment later Aunt Minna appeared in the doorway.

13

They stood for several seconds looking at one another. It was Minna who finally broke the silence.

'So you know,' she said.

Ellen shook her head. 'No, I wish I did,' she said. 'It's all so confusing. Aunt Minna, what does it mean? Why do you have these weapons stored here?'

With a deep sigh, Minna said, 'Come inside.'

Ellen stood her ground. She did not mean to be put off. 'No, I insist upon an explanation.'

'And you shall have it, but there's no need for us to stand down here where it's damp and musty. Come along. No one's going to empty the place while we're gone, if that's what you're thinking.'

It was so exactly what Ellen had been thinking that she blushed guiltily, and followed her aunt up the stairs, back to the fresh air of the garden.

'I'm sworn not to repeat any of this,' Minna began when they were seated in the den, 'but you've learned so much, it would be dangerous not to tell you the rest. Dawson was right, I suppose, I shouldn't have had you come here.'

'I'm very glad you did.'

Her aunt smiled a little. 'Yes, someone had to care about you, and I thought it would be better for you here. But I hadn't counted on your ferreting things out the way you have.'

She paused, jutting out her chin determinedly. 'It started almost two years ago. Dawson Elliot had made my acquaintance in researching that book of his. He's a charming man, a gentleman. There are too few of that sort about these days. We became friends.'

Ellen had her own opinion of Dawson's charm. In her opinion he turned it on and off all too easily, but she thought it best not to upset her aunt just now by criticizing Dawson, and remained silent.

'After a time, Dawson began to see that our thinking was alike on many points. It seemed to him that I might be not only

208

interested in something he was involved with, but useful to it also. Mind you, this wasn't an all-at-once proposition. He sounded me out on it very carefully, and there were others whose approval he needed before he could say anything directly to me. This was a life and death matter, you see, for thousands of people.'

'Surely you don't mean that literally.'

'I do indeed. What was involved were not just many lives, but the freedom of an entire nation. Can't you guess where this is leading?'

'No.' Ellen felt very thick-headed.

'You didn't study your geography very well in school,' Minna scolded. 'If you had, you'd know that by water we're very near a country that does not enjoy the freedoms we take for granted here.'

'Cuba,' Ellen said, the truth suddenly dawning on her. In her mind's eye she saw a map, and really that Cuba was indeed near. When people thought of that island, they always thought of Florida. But beyond Florida, Savannah was virtually the next port along the seaboard.

'Exactly. Surely there's no need for me

to go into the history of that unfortunate island.'

'There was an invasion — the Bay of Pigs, wasn't it?'

'A farce. Stupidly planned, a guaranteed failure.'

'But how does all this concern you?' She had not thought of her aunt as politically active.

Minna sat back in her chair and folded her hands on her lap. She had a triumphant look on her face, as if she had just scored an important victory.

'There's going to be another invasion of Cuba,' she said. 'A real one this time, not another charade like the last time. My dear, I give you my word, within a matter of weeks, Cuba will be free.'

Ellen was speechless. Never in her wildest dreams, not even at Lawndale, where wild dreams were the order of the day, had she imagined anything of this sort.

'The weapons in the cellar . . . ?' she said finally.

'Are for the invasion. Those and many more.'

'You don't mean the invasion is actually going to be launched from here?'

'Well, not from this house exactly, but from . . . ' She paused. 'From somewhere near here. It was necessary to bypass Florida after that last fiasco. There are too many people there watching everything. But here, no one would notice.'

Almost no one, Ellen thought. She was in a quandary. Should she tell Minna about Ken? At least now she understood his presence here and believed he was what he had said — but what should she do? Her aunt was involved in something quite beyond her expectations. And, yes, certainly dangerous.

'With access to the water, this house was perfect as a storage depot,' Minna said. 'You can see how beautifully it fitted into the scheme once Dawson and I had met.'

Or before, Ellen thought, but did not say. 'But, aunt, how could you have gotten involved in this? Or why?'

'Because it's important,' Minna said sharply, her eyes flashing. But after a moment her manner softened somewhat and she said, in a more kindly tone, 'We Southerners know what it's like to be subjugated, to have another's will imposed upon you. Anyway, these men, the ones who wanted to launch the invasion, were underdogs. They want to free their country, and Uncle Sam wanted no part of them. They are outcasts here and there. When you talk to them, you'll see. Your heart will go out to them as mine did.'

Ellen smiled despite herself. She could not help being a little touched by the old woman's attitude, involving herself in a dangerous plot because she was a champion of the underdog, the lost cause. The motivations that had brought her to invite Ellen here when others didn't want her.

'You've put yourself in rather a dangerous position,' she said aloud.

'Perhaps. But it's nearly over. The invasion will be launched within the next few days. Once it's done, a fait accompli, the danger will be past. There's nothing anyone can do then to prevent it.'

'There's still time now to prevent it.'

'You are the only one who knows, apart

from those of us active in the planning. And I forbid you to try to spoil this.' Her eyes were determined.

Ellen did not waver before that forceful gaze, however. She had to extricate her aunt from this scheme before Minna really got into trouble.

'If I thought I had to interfere to prevent you for causing yourself great grief, I wouldn't hesitate to do so,' she said. Minna opened her mouth angrily, but Ellen went on without waiting for her reply.

'As it is, I needn't do anything. I'm not the only one who knows, you see.'

'Who else?' Minna demanded.

'Ken Parker. He's an agent for the U.S. Government. He's been watching you and this house. He already knows what's afoot, I think.'

Minna got to her feet and made a gesture of annoyance. 'Dawson was right. He said that man wasn't to be trusted. Blast, now what should I do? I suppose you've been helping him to spy on us?' She turned angrily upon her niece.

'I'm afraid that wasn't necessary. He's

managed to do all right without any help from me.'

Minna was fairly beside herself. 'If Dawson were only here. He must know of this at once. Something will have to be done immediately.'

'There is one thing you can do.'

Minna whirled about. 'What is that?'

'You could talk to Ken.'

She might have spoken an obscene phrase, Minna was so shocked at the suggestion. 'If that was meant to be facetious . . . '

'But it wasn't. It can't harm anything after all. I mean, Ken already knows. You might be able to make him see your point of view. Or he might convert you to his way of thinking.'

Minna scoffed at the idea of anyone's changing her mind — but the former suggestion had merit. 'Yes,' she said after a pause, 'You're right. I will talk to him. When I've made him see what a great thing this is, how noble and heroic, I'm sure he'll agree to give us no interference.'

Ellen thought that unlikely, but she did want the two of them to meet and discuss this business. She had a hope, however slim, that Ken could dissuade her aunt from continuing this game of hers. She could see that there was nothing evil or wicked in Minna's involvement, but she realized too that her aunt did not fully comprehend the danger to herself.

'We can go see him now,' she said.

Minna came with her eagerly. Her own mind had leapt far ahead. If the United States Government could be persuaded to help — even surreptitiously — if she could accomplish that, wouldn't Dawson be floored?

14

It was with some surprise that Ken opened his door and found both Ellen and her aunt there. At first he could only stand and look from one to the other.

'May we come in?' Ellen asked.

'Of course.' He gestured them inside.

Minna was blunt. 'There's no use beating around the bush,' she said. 'I'll come right to the point. I found Ellen digging around in the cellar of my house. She had learned something I had not intended for her to learn. In the course of our subsequent conversation, she informed me that you are an agent for the United States Government.'

Ken gave Ellen an angry look but Minna did not give him time to say anything. 'She told me that,' she went on, 'because she thought it might be useful for you and I to get together.'

Ken looked a little uncertain. 'Are you telling me,' he asked when she paused, 'that you want to talk?'

'Young man, I am talking. What I've come for is to get your cooperation.'

He took a deep breath and looked at Ellen. She only smiled in return. She knew he was thinking this was quite unusual, but she had done all she could do. It was up to the two of them now.

'Look,' he said, 'you'd better start at the beginning.'

'How much do you already know?' Minna asked.

'Some. I know that there's a planned invasion of Cuba, and that your house is involved in it.'

She nodded. 'So you were getting awfully close, then. Well, yes, there is an invasion planned. Not some silly distraction, but a real invasion, with men and arms. We mean to liberate Cuba. We meant to do it without the U.S. Government finding out until it was done. But if you're already this close, I suppose the best thing is to make a deal. If you could help us . . . or failing that, simply see to it that there was no interference, it would make things much easier.'

'I don't have the authority to do anything like that. I was sent here to learn the details of the plan, if I could, and to stop the invasion.'

'Then you'll have to hold up on your report until after the invasion has been launched.'

Ken looked slightly amused. 'I'm afraid, Miss Miles, I can't do that either.'

'Then talk to your superior.' She spoke like a woman determined to have things her way.

Ken was thoughtful for a moment. 'Let me get this straight. If I bring my superior here, to talk to you, will you tell him all the details of this invasion?'

She considered the proposition for a moment. It meant betraying her promise to tell no one — but the government was so close to the full plan, anyway, and if she could persuade them, it would be so much the better.

'Very well,' she said, 'I'll tell him everything I know.'

'When is this invasion taking place?' When she hesitated, he said, 'I just want to know I actually have time to contact my chief. Otherwise, I'll just end up with egg on my face.'

'Not for a week.'

There was a moment of silence. Then, with a sigh, he said, 'This is highly irregular, but, all right, it's a deal. You go home and wait. I'll bring my chief there.'

He knew Nielsen was going to think he had flipped his wig. This was not the way these things were ordinarily done. On the other hand, his assignment had been to learn the details of this planned invasion, and here was the old woman, offering them on a gold platter, in return for a chance to talk to Nielsen. From his point of view, it couldn't be simpler.

'I shall return home and wait for you,' Minna said. 'Are you coming, Ellen?'

'In a minute. You go ahead.'

Minna looked disapprovingly at the two of them, but she went out and closed the door loudly after herself.

'Thank you for not laughing at her,' Ellen said to Ken. 'I know this all sounds silly, but she's serious about it, darling.'

'It is serious, more serious than she realizes.'

'I'm sorry I had to tell her who you were.'

'You did the right thing. This may have saved us a lot of work. Look, you go up to the house, keep an eye on her. The main thing now is, don't let her talk to Dawson Elliot. Hit her on the head with something if you have to, but keep her on ice and out of his way until I get back here with my boss. Got it?'

'I'll go right home. But I don't know how long Dawson will be out. You'd better hurry.'

He was already phoning when she slipped from the cottage and took the path back to Minna's.

* * *

Dawson Elliot stood at the steps leading down into the cellar, staring at the burning light bulb, the open doors, the evidence that someone had been here and had left in a hurry. He went into the farthest corner and saw that the radio equipment there was untouched. Not, then, someone bent on mischief or sabotage.

He heard the sound of footsteps above. He fell into a crouch, grabbing his gun from inside his jacket. A shadow fell across the opening.

'Dawson, are you there?' Minna called down.

He hurried up the steps, his usually handsome face ugly with anger. 'What is the meaning of this?' he demanded. 'Who's been prowling around down here? And what were you doing out, leaving things open like this, for anyone to come in and find them?'

She seemed to take no notice of his anger. Her face was bright with enthusiasm. 'Dawson,' she said in a quick, eager voice, 'I've got something to tell you.'

He listened in stony silence while she told her story. When she talked about the bargain she had struck with Ken Parker, his scowl deepened, and by the time she had finished, even she could see he was anything but pleased.

'I must say,' she paused after her

lengthy monologue, 'you don't look very happy, considering that I might have guaranteed the success of our little plan.'

He had been biting his tongue while he listened. Now his anger erupted. 'You old fool,' he said with such vehemence that Minna was too dumbfounded even to respond to the insult. 'The last thing I want is for the United States Government to cooperate, as you put it. You should have talked to me before you did anything. I could have handled Parker, just as I handled that fool girl he sent over here.'

'But, Dawson, if the government could be persuaded to help us, we could succeed beyond our fondest dreams.'

'Succeed?' His voice was a cold sneer. 'You don't even know what success means. Success will be the failure of this little invasion.'

'Failure? But we can't fail. We . . . '

He threw his head back and laughed. 'You're mad. Did you think for a moment that a handful of boats and forty or fifty untrained men would be enough to take over Cuba? Yes, they'll fail. That was the idea from the beginning.'

'But I've talked to these men. They mean to liberate Cuba.'

'Oh, yes, they think they're going to do that. They think they have a chance. They're fools too. They will lose. But I will win. The people for whom I work will win.'

She looked as white as the moon above. 'But, I thought you cared for Cuba.'

He laughed again. 'Cuba? Nobody cares for Cuba. It's the United States that's important. It's the U.S. my people want to see fail, to look foolish — just as they did the last time. Cuba is important only in helping that to happen. That's why the Cuban army will be waiting when those men land on the island. Another American-backed invasion.'

Minna gasped. 'They're going into a trap?'

'Yes.'

'It was all a scheme to discredit this country, and I've helped you.' She seemed to recover from her shock. She drew her shoulders back. 'But it won't work now, because Mr. Parker knows about it, and he and his superior will be here soon. I shall tell them the truth, the whole truth.'

'You'll tell them nothing. And Mr. Parker will be too late. We're going down into the cellar now, you and I, and send the message that will begin the invasion tonight.'

'But they won't be ready.'

'Don't you see, that won't matter? They're going to lose anyway.'

★   ★   ★

Standing just inside the door to the library, Ellen held her breath for fear Dawson would hear it. She had nearly run out into the garden without realizing he was there. Luckily, the sound of his voice had stopped her in time.

She must tell Ken of this change in plans. He would know what to do. Her breath in her throat, she began to back on tiptoe toward the hall. She reached the door without incident and opened it, gritting her teeth when it squeaked. But the two in the moon garden were too far away to hear. She slipped out and hurried across the terrace.

If only he were still there.

★ ★ ★

Ken stepped onto the flagstone outside his door, frowning. He was thinking ahead to his interview with Nielsen. He knew well enough how Nielsen would view the idea of cooperating with Ellen and the old lady.

Parker himself, though, was convinced that Ellen's aunt had been used as a dupe. He was sure she had been telling the truth so far as she knew it. All he had to do was convince his chief of that and to persuade him that it would be better for them to tell Minna Miles the truth and work through her than to work against her.

He ran up the steps and got into his car, reaching for the ignition, then paused. Something flickered at the back of his mind. He had an urge to go back to the cottage, but for what he didn't know. He tried to think if he had forgotten anything. He put his hand on the door to open it.

Nielsen was waiting, however, and Nielsen did not like to wait.

★   ★   ★

Ellen was almost to the door of the cottage when she heard a car's engine come to life on the street above. It was his, she was sure. She bypassed the cottage and ran up the steps, praying she would get there before he pulled away.

She was too late. As she reached the street, twin red lights reached the corner, turned, and were gone.

There was nothing for her to do but wait till he returned. She would wait at the cottage to be certain she saw him as soon as possible.

She let herself in. Remembering his gun and the way he had come in the last time, she left her key in the lock and the door slightly ajar, so he would know she was here.

She was too restless to read. She found his hairbrush in the bathroom and, letting her hair down, began to brush it.

She had not been there long when she heard footsteps on the terrace. Ken must have forgotten something and come back for it.

The footsteps paused as they came near the door. She imagined what he must be thinking, wondering who was inside. She got up from the couch and started lightly across the room.

'Darling, it's all right,' she called. 'It's only me.'

She threw the door open, smiling her welcome, but the smile froze on her face. It was not Ken, but Dawson who stood outside.

She felt a perfect fool. She could think of nothing to say or do. If she could flee inside, slam the door, lock it — but there wasn't time enough for that, he was too close.

'May I come in?' he asked.

'Mr. Parker isn't here.'

'So I gathered.' He came forward, so that she could only step aside and let him come in. She pointedly left the door wide open and remained near it.

He did not even seem to notice. He lit a cigarette, glancing around. 'Nice place. A bit small for my tastes, but functional-looking.' His eyes, sliding around the room, came to rest on her. 'You and Parker have gotten rather intimate, haven't you?'

She stiffened and blushed.

'I don't know that we're so intimate.'

'You've rather made yourself at home. And the term 'darling' suggests intimacy to me. Come off it, my dear. You know, I don't give a hoot if he's your lover.'

She glanced briefly at him. He was digging, trying to confirm what he thought he knew. She wished she could hide her feelings better. She suddenly felt utterly transparent.

'It's none of my business anyway,' he said. 'It's no use pretending anymore, you know.

'What do you mean?'

'The cat's out of the bag, isn't it? Parker knows what we've been up to. Minna says you've been helping him.'

'Not really.' He did not seem per-turbed, and it came to her suddenly then

— he did not know she had overheard that conversation between him and Minna. He thought he had no reason to worry. All he had to do was keep her occupied for an hour or so. That was why he had come, to stall her, or even to stall Ken, until his invasion had been launched. So far as he knew, they would think they had at least a week to prevent it.

His ignorance also meant, however, that she had nothing to fear from him, as long as he did not know what she knew. She was no immediate threat to him. If she could only keep him from suspecting . . .

She tried a smile. 'I hope you aren't angry with me. I know what you're doing is for a good cause, but I was so worried that my aunt might be getting herself into trouble.'

'I can see your point of view. And maybe after all, you'll prove to be right. That's why I came up. I thought I ought to talk to Parker, and even this chief of his. I was hoping we might set up a meeting for, say, tomorrow. Minna seems to be questioning the wisdom of our scheme. If she and Parker can convince me, I'll be the first to scuttle the whole idea.'

He sounded so convincing. If she hadn't heard him herself a short while before, she would think he was sincere. She could imagine him giving Ken the same song-and-dance. Arranging a meeting for, 'say, tomorrow,' when it would be too late.

Well, all she had to do for now was to pretend to believe him.

'I'm glad you see it that way,' she said.

'To tell the truth, I'm glad we can stop all the pretending. It hurt me to have to deceive you, you know. Tell you that you were imagining things. I saw how it worried you. I'd have told you the truth from the beginning if Minna hadn't insisted we couldn't.'

'I wish you had. It would have saved me a great deal of grief.'

'I'm really very fond of you, you know.' He came a step closer.

Instinctively she took a step back, and regretted it at once. She saw that he resented it, but he came no closer.

'I'll tell you what,' he said, smiling again. 'Your ghost ship is at the landing at this very moment. Let's stroll down and have a look, shall we?'

Her heart pushed its way up into her throat. 'I ought to wait for Ken.'

'We'll only be down at the landing. And a few minutes can't make much difference, can they?'

All the difference in the world, she thought, but aloud she said, 'No, I suppose not.'

'I feel I owe it to you, to sort of make amends. Come along.' He went toward the door.

She felt trapped. If she refused to go with him, he might begin to suspect why. And if he knew she had learned of the change in his plans . . .

'I'll just put Ken's hairbrush back,' she said.

She went into the bathroom. Her eyes darted over the countertop, looking for something with which to leave Ken a message. She started back through the dressing room and saw a pencil and a note pad atop the dresser.

'I think I'll borrow one of Ken's jackets.' She swung the closet door wide to block his view of the dressing room, and wrote, in a rapid scrawl, 'At landing w/Dawson. Invasion changed. Tonight.'

It was all she had time for. She gave the clothes in the closet a shake, rattling hangers. 'Now, where ... ah, here's something.'

From the other room, Dawson watched in the mirror over the dresser, saw her pretense of searching the closet and the hastily written note.

He was smiling when she emerged from the dressing room, a big, plaid shirt-jacket over her shoulders.

He took her arm as they started down the path. They had reached the clearing when he clapped his hand over his pocket and said, 'Blast, I've forgotten my lighter. I must have left it up at Parker's.'

'I think you smoke too much anyway,' she said with a hoarse little laugh.

'I'll run back for it. Is the door locked?'

'No, I left it open. But I can go.'

'Now that is what I would call reverse

232

chivalry. Don't you budge an inch. I can run up there and back in a minute.'

He was gone before she could think of any way to dissuade him. He won't go into the dressing room, she told herself, trying to remain calm. He hadn't been in there, so there was no reason for him to think he'd left his lighter there. He'll go in, see his lighter, and come right back.

He was right back, too. It seemed as if he had been gone only seconds, and then he was hurrying down the path, and from his unconcerned manner, she knew he had not discovered her note. She breathed a little easier.

Dawson put his arm about her waist. She willed herself not to shrink from him this time and even leaned against him a little.

His other hand went briefly to his pocket, and the crumpled piece of paper there.

15

Her phantom ship looked very ghostlike indeed in the pale moonlight, with not a light aboard. It was surprisingly small, too. She knew little about things nautical, but she guessed where it went to and came from was not very distant.

At first glimpse it appeared deserted, but then she saw people moving about on it and suddenly, before they had even reached the landing, someone came along the path behind them. She started, but Dawson had a firm grip on her.

'It's all right,' he said, 'just some of the men taking a load from the cellars.'

Two men went past them carrying boxes from the cellar. She knew full well why they were being loaded now, but she couldn't resist seeing how Dawson meant to explain it.

'If you think you might be persuaded to give your scheme up, isn't it silly to do all this work now?' she asked.

'We don't know yet that I'm going to. Besides, even if I do, these people don't know that yet and this pickup was already arranged. If I called it off now it would raise a lot of questions. I'm not the big cheese in this venture, you know.'

You are as far as these men know, she thought. As they passed, the two men gave him the kind of wary respect reserved for someone who is in charge.

The men handed their boxes off to others onboard the ship and started back the way they had come.

'Excuse me a moment,' Dawson said. He left her on the landing and went after them. For a moment she thought that maybe she could escape, but the only route open to her was right by the three men on the path. She should have bolted, perhaps, in that minute or so he'd left her alone in the clearing — but to where? He would only have followed her to Minna's. No, she had to continue this charade until Ken returned and found her note.

She tried to hear what Dawson was discussing with those two men, but the lapping of the water against the pilings muffled the conversation. They seemed to be arguing.

Apparently Dawson had his way. He came back to her. The other two remained where they had been. One of them lit a cigarette, which indicated they might be there for a while.

She was pointedly admiring the ship when Dawson rejoined her. 'It's lovely,' she said. 'May we go aboard?'

'I'd intended just that.' He took her arm and she leaned against him slightly as he led the way up the ramp to the boat.

The deck was stacked with boxes and empty of people, but as they stepped on deck, a stocky man in black trousers and black sweater emerged from the cabin door.

'Almost ready,' he said to Dawson. He had a thick accent that she guessed was Cuban. She recognized him at once. He was the man she'd seen peering in the window at night.

'The rest won't be coming,' Dawson said. 'There isn't time.'

The man in black looked toward the two men on land, but Dawson said,

'They'll stay with me. I'll need a couple of hands. You're to go on to the island. I'll join you there in a short while.'

Ellen's ears tingled. The island? Surely that must be the launching site. If she knew where it was, could find its exact location . . .

'Oh, Dawson,' she said, turning on him with bright eyes and a forced smile. 'You don't mean you have your own private island out there?'

He smiled down at her. 'As a matter of fact, we do have. Didn't your aunt tell you that? It's not much of an island, more of an overgrown sandbar, but it serves our purposes. Would you like to see it?'

It was even easier than she had hoped. 'I'd love to. Can we? Could I run over with you when you go?'

Dawson looked amused. 'There's no need for you to have to wait around until I'm ready. You'll sail with Captain Rivera here. Captain, Miss Miles will be sailing with you.'

She had a frightful premonition of what he was leading up to. She tried to slip free of his arm, but he held her firmly.

'Dawson,' she said, still trying to seem enthusiastic despite the fear that was making her numb, 'I'm in no rush. I'd rather make the trip with you, really. Not that I have anything against the captain, but I thought it would be so pleasant, you and I and all this moonlight.'

She was talking too fast, and unconvincingly and she knew it. He looked more amused than ever.

He said, coldly, 'You're a rotten actress, my pet.'

'I don't understand.'

'Don't you?' He was forcing her toward the cabin door. She tried to drag her feet but of course it was no good.

'Dawson!' she put all the shocked indignation she could muster into the exclamation.

'Shut up.' He yanked open the cabin door. A group of men, perhaps a half dozen, gave them curious looks.

Dawson snapped something at them in Spanish. The men jumped up and began to file past her out of the cabin. She struggled in Dawson's embrace, but he held her firmly.

'I thought you'd prefer a little privacy for the voyage,' he told her. 'I don't want you to think I'm a brute.'

He gave her a hard shove so that she nearly fell. By the time she'd gotten her balance, the door was shut and locked.

'Dawson!' She ran to the door and rattled the knob, and pounded on the wood. There was no reply from outside.

Shaking with anger and fear, she turned from the door and saw a scrap of yellow paper on the floor. When she picked it up and smoothed it out, she saw it was the note she had left for Ken.

★ ★ ★

Dawson gave Rivera his instructions, making the man repeat them to be sure he had them right. You couldn't be too careful with these fools. They hardly ever got anything right. And to think they actually deluded themselves that they could stage a counter-revolution and take over Cuba.

It was a great joke, except that it

worked so well for him and his masters in the Middle East. He was sure to get a commendation for making the United States look so inept on the world stage.

Of course the United States would disclaim any responsibility or even knowledge, but that would sound pretty lame — particularly since he already had one C.I.A. employee ready to confess to the opposite. It would cost them a minor agent, of course, but the man really wasn't very good anyway.

He rejoined the men at the bottom of the path and ordered them to follow him. Just before they went into the trees, he looked back at the boat in the water, making ready to slip away with Ellen aboard. He was really sorry about that part of it.

Blast it, what was there about that girl anyway? She wasn't all that pretty. He had personally slit much lovelier throats than hers. And yet for the first time he really regretted having signed someone's death warrant. He would have liked to carry this business off without having to hurt her, but that was impossible now. He was truly sorry this one had to die.

He shook his head. That was dangerous thinking. 'Let's go,' he said aloud. The two men were waiting, watching him. They followed him into the darkness.

16

They were moving. She could not see out because the windows had what looked like black oilcloth taped over them, but the boat swayed under her and lifted with a creak of timber at each wave.

She could almost follow their progress, from the gentle cove into the river and, after a time, into the sea. She knew they must have reached the ocean because the lifting and falling had gotten more energetic. The boat was alive and under sail.

There wasn't much to see inside the cabin. Under the windows on each side were settees with cushions in cracked vinyl. On one side was a wooden table, attached to floor and wall and hinged so it could be dropped down out of the way. A light fixture hung above it, unlighted. What light there was came instead from a hanging lantern. There was a little kitchen, pretty much devoid of equipment. This boat was not used for pleasure trips.

She sat down at the table and tried to think. Ken would be home soon, if he wasn't there already. What would he do? His superior would likely want to talk to her and Minna, so they would go to Minna's house and find that she was gone, and . . . and what? Short of telepathic perception, they could hardly guess where she was.

Would Minna tell them? Did she even know? She was certain Minna would never have agreed to this, having her kidnapped. But Dawson probably would not tell her.

Minna did know about the boat, though. She would know it had come and gone from the landing. If Ellen were discovered missing, she would surely connect the two facts in her mind. And she had quarreled with Dawson, she had seen how he had used her as a dupe, so their 'partnership' would not prevent her from speaking out.

So there was some hope, however slim. They might come after her and find her. She must cling to that. There was nothing else she could do.

She had no idea how far they had traveled before she heard a heavy step outside the cabin door. It was unlocked noisily and in a gust of cold air the captain came in.

He paused just inside the door, looking at her. She saw his dark eyes slip away from her face and run downward over her body. He shut the door and slipped the bolt into the latch. Its faint click was like the clanging of an alarm bell to her ears.

He went to the kitchen and opened a drawer. She threw a glance in the direction of the door, but he was closer to it than she. And even if she reached it and got outside, there was nowhere for her to go. There were other men up there, and nothing else but the ocean.

He brought a piece of blank paper and a pencil over to her, clapping them heavily down upon the table. 'You are to sign your name to this,' he said.

She looked up at him, wide-eyed. They wanted her signature on a note they would compose later. What kind of a note could it be? A confession of some sort? Or a suicide note?

'I won't do it. You can't make me sign it.'

'He has the old woman at the house.' The captain's voice was emotionless, matter-of-fact. These were mere business details. His business just happened to be very unsavory. 'I am to radio him and tell him if you have signed or not. If not . . . ' He shrugged. There was no need to be more explicit. They both knew what he was implying.

She took a deep breath. All things considered, it would be easy to make her suicide convincing — a young woman who only a short time before had been released from a mental hospital and who had been having delusions since.

But if she didn't sign, would Dawson carry out the threat to Minna?

Probably. He had little to lose at this time. Treason, kidnapping, her murder, which surely they must be contemplating — how much difference could Minna's murder make?

'I need time to think.' Her skin felt as if

it were crawling under his gaze.

'There is no time. You must sign now.' He poked a finger at the paper.

With trembling hand she picked up the pencil and hurriedly scrawled her signature on the paper. He snatched it up, examining it as if he thought she might have tried some sort of trick, and stuffed it into the pocket of his shirt.

But he did not go. He continued to stare down at her. She saw his forehead had broken out in sweat. He licked his lips nervously.

'Now,' he said, but whatever he meant to say was interrupted by a knocking at the door and a flood of Spanish. The captain listened, said something back, and listened again. He looked displeased.

So suddenly that she hadn't time to anticipate the move, he leaned across her to the lantern and turned the wick down. The cabin went black, beyond mere darkness. It was the blackness of the pit.

His hand touched her shoulder. She gave a terrified little gasp and shrank helplessly away from his touch.

'I've never been so furious in my life.' Minna looked as if with very little provocation she could leap across the space that separated her from Dawson and savagely throttle him.

He, on the other hand, looked quite unconcerned. 'You must calm yourself,' he said, sipping from a glass of wine. 'It isn't good for you to get excited. Anyway, I want you composed in case the police should come later.'

'They'll come. Having those beasts of yours keep me from a phone won't prevent that.'

'They may come, yes. In which case, we must get clear what you will tell them.'

'I'm going to tell them the truth. Everything. I don't care if they throw me into a dungeon for the rest of my life. I'll have the satisfaction of knowing you'll be in one as well.'

'My dear Minna, I have no intention of either of us rotting away in a cell somewhere. If you will do as I tell you, everything shall be all right.'

'It won't.'

'That would be most unfortunate for your niece.'

Her eyes, suddenly wide, flicked toward the upstairs.

'I have her,' Dawson said. 'She's on the *Liza* right now, on her way to the island, in the company of Captain Rivera.'

'That dog? If anything happens to her, I will personally — '

'Nothing will. If you cooperate.'

'You wouldn't harm her?'

He smiled and said nothing.

In her head, her clamoring thoughts indicted her for her foolishness. She looked at Dawson and her eyes filled with hate and loathing.

'The authorities may not come tonight,' Dawson said. 'In which case we have nothing to fear. By morning it will be far too late. But if they should come tonight, we must delay them as long as possible. We need an hour or two, that's all. Now, I will tell you how you must act and what you must say.'

She sank into her chair, numb with the fear of what might happen to Ellen. She could scarcely make out what Dawson was saying. His voice droned on and on.

⋆   ⋆   ⋆

'This is the damndest thing I ever let myself get talked into,' Nielsen was saying as he followed his agent into the little yellow cottage. 'A meeting with two of the very people we're supposed to be watching. I ought to send you to the happy farm.'

Ken tried not to react to the tirade. He had been hearing it since he had met Nielsen at the waterfront and told him what he wanted. But at least he had persuaded Nielsen to come back here with him. If Nielsen could pry the details out of the old woman, they could wrap this whole business up. At the same time, Minna's cooperation could make the difference between prison for her or spending the rest of her years free.

He had to accomplish the latter, for Ellen's sake. She would never forgive him if her aunt went to prison as a result of his investigation.

'You're sure this old lady knows all the details?' Nielsen asked. He saw the bottle of Scotch on the kitchen counter and went to help himself to a drink.

'Everything. But she thinks Elliot is sincerely trying to liberate the Cubans. I couldn't tell her the true story without authority. But you can. Once she knows what he's really up to, I'm convinced she'll cooperate. She can take us right to the base they're using.'

Nielsen considered that for a moment. 'They've been storing arms in her house, right?'

'And taking it out by boat. They must be just about due for another pickup, too. If we set it up right, we could catch them in the act.'

Nielsen weighed the prospects. They had known boats were coming and going from the landing at the old lady's house. Right now he had a boat patrolling the waters just off the coast, looking for any suspicious vessels. He could bring it in, just up the river. If a pickup was attempted, they could block off the river and have their fish in a net.

He took his cell phone from his pocket and dialed a number. When a cautious voice answered, Nielsen barked an identifying number and without waiting for confirmation, said, 'Have Jack bring that boat of his in, right now. I want it as close as he can get to the landing down here without being conspicuous, and I want him to stand by for action.'

He disconnected and turned back to Parker. 'Now, you get that girl and that old lady over here. And, buster, this had better be good.'

17

Ellen sat shivering in the darkness. She had gotten some kind of reprieve. He had put out the lantern and she heard him moving through the inky darkness. The bolt slid back, the door opened, letting a little moonlight spill into the cabin.

'You,' he said menacingly, 'make no noise.' Then he was gone, closing the door, and she was in blackness once more.

She was too weak to do anything for a minute or two but sit and tremble. There was no doubt in her mind of what he had been intending. Not only was there that horror to contemplate, but it told her more plainly than words that Dawson meant her to die. He wouldn't have given permission for anything of that sort if he'd meant her to tell of it later.

Thank God for whatever had distracted Rivera and given her at least a temporary reprieve. That it was temporary she had no doubt, but it gave her some hope. Somewhere in this cabin she might find a weapon, perhaps in the kitchen. Even if they weren't equipped for cooking, they surely must have some sort of utensils on hand. If not a knife, then even a heavy pan or a bottle — anything was preferable to sitting helplessly and waiting for him to . . .

She had an idea. She got up, bumping her leg in the darkness, and felt her way, moving as quickly as she could, to the door. Yes, just as she had remembered, there was a bolt on the inside of the door. She slid it into place.

She leaned against the door, heaving a sigh of relief. If the bolt were strong enough, it would keep her safe from him until . . . but there was no 'until'. Even if he couldn't get in, sooner or later she would have to come out, and he would be waiting. He could even let her starve to death in here if he chose, or scuttle the boat with her in it.

She heard movement and noise on the deck. It sounded like boxes being dragged across the boards. What was it, she suddenly wondered, that had so alarmed Rivera that he'd abandoned his plans for her?

She felt her way back to the table. Kneeling on one of the vinyl seats, she ran her fingers along the wall, to the window. The tape holding the oilcloth was fresh and held to the wood firmly. She got a fingernail under one edge. It was hard to manage without seeing, but at last she got a piece peeled back to where she could get a hold on it. She tore the covering away from the window and peered out.

At first she saw nothing but undulating water. She strained her eyes as if she could send the very urgency of her dilemma across the waves.

She saw it, then, gray in the moonlight — another boat. A powerful-looking launch riding low in the water, swift and menacing. It leaned to one side and she realized it was turning toward them.

Hope sprang up within her. If she could somehow signal them . . . the lantern, of course. She reached for it before she even thought, she would need a match to relight it.

She bit hard at her lip. There surely must be matches somewhere. They had lit the lantern before, hadn't they? But where in the darkness were they?

She looked out the window again, wondering if it would do her any good to yell. The other boat looked so far away. It was moving at an angle toward them, but slowly. Its present course would carry it by this boat without bringing it near enough to hear her.

No, she must find matches. The moonlight from the window gave at least a pale light. She got to her feet and began to feel her way cautiously toward the kitchen.

★　★　★

The other boat had been headed for the mouth of the river, as instructed. But the dark sailing ship had caught the eye of Jack, the man at the wheel, and he had swung the launch closer for a look.

'What do you think?' the man beside him asked.

'Looks suspicious as hell. No lights, running like the devil was after it. It might be our baby.'

'Might be. We'd just about have to board it to know, though. We might be asking for trouble.'

Jack hesitated. He'd throttled the launch down until they were barely moving. They were a hundred yards or so from the other boat.

He wasn't thinking about the trouble they might stir up if they went in for a look. He was thinking of the delay. Something was up back in Savannah. Nielsen's instructions had been clear. Come in and wait for action.

'We'd better let it go,' he said aloud, revving the engine. 'When Nielsen says to do something, he means now.'

He gave the wheel a turn. The launch leaned and surged forward. In the distance he could see the lights of Savannah.

'Hey, wait a minute,' the man beside him said, putting a hand on his arms. 'Someone just put a light on in the cabin of that boat.'

Jack smiled. 'That settles it. If they were our boys, they wouldn't be flashing any lights, would they?'

His companion was thoughtful, looking back at the sailing ship, now farther and farther away. He'd always trusted his instincts. He'd heard Nielsen say once you had to have a nose for trouble if you were going to be successful in their line of work. And his nose itched like something was amiss on that boat.

Jack apparently didn't think so, though. They were picking up speed. He seemed to have decided what they should do, and he was the one in charge.

'I guess you're right,' the man said, but his nose itched something fierce.

* * *

They were going away. She had found a book of paper matches in the third drawer she searched. The cover felt damp, but the first match she tried lit despite her shaking fingers. After it had gone out, however, she realized her mistake. There were only three in the book. She had two left.

She stumbled back to the lantern and, after what seemed an eternity, found out how to open it. She struck a match and turned the wick up. The match sputtered and went out.

She took a deep breath, willing her hands steady, and struck the third and last match.

The wick caught, a tiny thread of fire running across its surface and then, as if joyfully discovering itself, leaping to brilliance. She swung the chimney down into place, lest she inadvertently put the flame out, and lifted the lantern toward the window, swinging it frantically in her hand.

She had been so absorbed in getting the lantern lit that she had not heard the noise when the nearby launch kicked up its engine and began to pull away. Now, looking from the window, she saw it was going away, the distance between the two boats rapidly increasing.

A wave of despair swept over her. Tears stung her eyes. They couldn't go away just like that. Surely they must have seen her light. If only she knew how to do an S.O.S., but there wasn't even time for that.

It was useless. She was trapped here, doomed. Any moment, now that the threat was leaving, the captain would return.

No, she could still look for a weapon. If nothing else, she had the lantern and . . . suddenly she knew what she must do. There was still one way she could signal that other boat, one distress signal they couldn't ignore.

With a wild yank she tore one of the curtains from the window. It was a coarse, burlap-like material. She opened the lantern and held the cloth to the flame. It caught fire at once. She held it to the second curtain and in an instant it was blazing too. Her fingers trembled as she unscrewed the base of the lantern and splashed the kerosene across the table, over the wood of the floor and the wall.

For a moment nothing happened. She stepped back from the burning curtains, the light playing in eerie patterns over her face.

With an odd whooshing sound, the spilled fuel caught fire too. Flames leapt upward, making the cabin's interior as bright as day. The wood of the table caught almost as quickly as the curtains had done. In mere seconds, the cabin was an inferno, the flames hungrily sweeping from place to place. She watched a closet door burst into flames.

It was a desperate gamble. If that other boat did not come back, she might very well go to the bottom of the ocean with Captain Rivera and his crew, but she would as soon that as the alternative.

The flames had been contained till now within the cabin, but she heard a shout from outside, and knew that they had spread beyond it. She went to the door, as far from the fire as she could get. Even there it was quickly growing hot. She had no way now of getting to the window to see if her desperate measure had worked and the other boat was coming back. She could only trust to providence.

Outside, men were shouting, feet

pounding. The door was unlocked and someone pushed against it, but the bolt held. She had to be certain the fire was going well. If they got it out too quickly, she was done for. If she waited too long, she would be trapped here.

The heat grew intense. She reached for the bolt and at once jerked her hand back. The metal was red-hot.

'Señorita!' It was the captain, yelling from outside. 'Señorita, open the door!'

She used the bottom of her skirt as a glove and with a quick movement slid the bolt back. At the same moment, she jumped aside.

The captain charged through the door, almost colliding with her. A crowd of men pushed in behind him. For the moment they had no eyes for her. They shared one thought, to put out that blazing fire.

She coughed and pushed her way through the men to the outside. Suddenly she was free, on the deck. She could see where the flames had already eaten through and were burning out here as well. Columns of smoke lifted heavenward.

She drank deeply of the cool, fresh air and stumbled toward the railing to look for that other boat. But she had gone no more than a few feet when she heard Captain Rivera yell, 'The girl? Where is the girl? Someone get her and hold on to her.'

The men clustered at the door looked around and saw her. Someone said something and three of them came toward her.

There was no time to get her bearings or to look for that other boat, not even time to think of the best course of action. There was only one way of escape open to her, one slim chance, and she took it.

She dashed to the rail, and clambered over. Someone grabbed her arm, but the boat lurched and the hand slipped from her. In the same instant, she half-dived, half-fell overboard, pitching into the sea.

18

She felt as if she must have swallowed half the ocean. She went down until she was sure she would touch the bottom, and the water was a dark weight that tried to crush her. She kicked and thrashed, and suddenly she was at the surface and could gasp at the night air greedily. The moving black surface of the ocean was punctuated with yellow and gold reflections from the burning boat.

She sank again, kicking out wildly in a panic for a second or two, before reason took hold of her. She lost a shoe, and remembered to kick the other off. Again she surfaced and this time when she opened her stinging eyes she was looking at the boat she had just escaped. Somehow she had gotten a considerable distance from it.

Pandemonium reigned there. Flames leapt skyward, dancing and swirling. Some of the men on deck were fighting the blaze, but it looked as if they were losing the fight. One and then another, and still another, followed her example and dove into the sea.

She treaded water. The sounds from the boat seemed to come between the waves that lifted and dropped her alternately. She recognized Captain Rivera at the tail and for a second or two she did not comprehend that he was holding a rifle. Something sounding like a hornet buzzed past her ear.

He was shooting at her. Of course he would want her dead. If they jumped ship and had to be rescued by strangers, their plan was delayed, maybe for years, but they could still hope to escape once they reached land — unless she were alive to tell her tale.

A second shot went somewhere off in the distance. She didn't wait to see how much closer he came with the third. A wave lifted her. She saw the captain as the wave crested and then he disappeared. The tips of the waves were white in the moonlight. She tried to swim, riding them as best she could. She was strong and healthy, but only a mediocre swimmer. She could not tell by the rolling water if she was making any progress or not, and she didn't dare pause to look back.

The sea suddenly turned glassy yellow. A searchlight had found her. She was afraid to dive, afraid she wouldn't come back to the surface. Her limbs were like lead.

Something splashed near by. A man surfaced seconds later and swam toward her. She was too tired to try to escape him.

'Don't struggle,' he said.

As if she could! She let his arms and the buoyant water carry her while she concentrated on breathing hard and deep. She drifted. The darkness seemed to deepen and she had a sensation of sinking. She thought he was drowning her, and her last thought was that it would take no great effort on his part.

★   ★   ★

She woke with a crashing pain in her lungs and someone bending over her. She opened her eyes with some effort and found herself looking at close range into a male face, one she didn't know.

'Easy,' he said, and, 'She's coming around.'

'Keep a gun on her.'

That woke her up. She lifted her head despite the pain. Several men stood around her. One of them did indeed have a gun trained on her.

'Can you sit up?'

'I think so,' she said falteringly. She made an effort. With his help she managed to get more or less vertical, with her legs curled under her. Someone brought a blanket and dropped it around her shoulders. She was still in her wet clothes, shivering and too dazed to think who these men were or why they had guns. Dawson's cohorts? Which meant she hadn't escaped after all.

'Can you talk?' One of the men asked.

She nodded, not really sure she could, but willing to try, if only they would allow her to huddle in this blanket for a time.

Someone thrust a big mug of hot coffee at her. She took it gratefully, spilling a little of it on the blanket. It burned her mouth, but it was easily the most delicious thing she had ever tasted.

'Are you the Miles girl?'

She nodded at the man who seemed to be in charge.

'Where were you headed in that boat?'

'I don't know.'

He looked as if he didn't believe her. 'How many men were on it?'

She shook her head. 'A dozen, maybe more.' She remembered the fire then, and asked, 'Is it — ?'

'It's gone.'

She blinked, remembering then that it had been loaded with guns and ammunition. Once the fire had spread to the wooden deck, the whole thing must have blown sky-high. She thought of the men who had been on board — only a short time before threats to her, and yet probably not genuinely evil men, with one or two exceptions. They had been patriots, fighting for their country's freedom, duped by Dawson just as Minna had been duped. And they had paid for that mistake with their lives.

'You must have been carrying quite a load on board,' the man said. 'It was like the Fourth of July out there for a few minutes.'

'Jack,' another voice said, 'we're almost at the landing.'

'Take it on by,' Jack said, 'till we're just out of sight.'

She suddenly realized where they must be. She saw the dark forms of trees gliding by the window. While she had been unconscious, they had slipped quietly into the river and were almost to Minna's landing.

Jack said, 'Andy, you scoot up to Parker's place when we get to the bank and see what he and Nielsen have cooking.'

'You're Ken's men,' she said, surprised.

'That's right,' Jack said.

She got unsteadily to her feet. 'But you can't go on by the landing. We've got to put in there. I've got to see Ken.'

'Our orders are to put up out of sight. I went way out on a limb taking time to come back and fish you out of the water. For all I know, we may already be too late.'

'You will be if you just sit and wait.'

He made an impatient gesture and started to turn from her but she caught his sleeve. 'Those men, the ones on the boat, they were taking me to some sort of island off the coast. They're planning to launch an invasion of Cuba from there.'

'We know all about that,' he said, but he was listening now with interest.

'But what you don't know is that they're planning to do it now, tonight. It may already be underway.'

Everything stopped on the boat. 'You're sure of this?' Jack asked.

'Yes. But Ken doesn't know. We've got to tell him. And my aunt . . . '

But Jack wasn't interested in hearing about her aunt. He turned toward the man at the wheel. 'Pull in at that landing,' he ordered. To the other men in the boat he said, 'Stay on board and be ready for anything.'

The engine cut back. The launch turned. The water here was smooth. There was a scraping of wood on wood and the boat bobbed as someone moved across the deck and jumped ashore.

Jack took her arm, not altogether gently. 'Come on, you're going up there with me, and by God you'd better be telling me the truth, because if you aren't I'll be out of a job.'

She came along with him gladly. A great deal more needed to be said. She hadn't yet warned him about the danger to Aunt Minna. But she had persuaded him to put in here and go up to the house with her. Ken would know what to do next.

They jumped from the boat onto the landing. Her legs were still a little shaky but the man with her seemed to have forgotten that she had nearly drowned only a short time before. He walked swiftly, with long strides, propelling her along with him, but she was as eager to reach the house as she was, and somehow she managed to match his pace.

Her clothes were mostly dry by now. She was shoeless, but the pine needles covered the ground like a thick carpet and made the going easier than it might have been.

He stumbled once and nearly fell. 'Let

me lead the way,' she said in a whisper. She sensed rather than saw his hesitation. 'I can't very likely outrun you.'

'I guess you're right. Okay, but no tricks.'

She ran lightly up the path, darted across the clearing, and they were in the trees once again. She paused at the terrace. Aunt Minna's house was brightly lit.

Jack took command again. 'Stay beside me,' he said and quickly crossed the terrace, to the French doors off the library. One of those doors was slightly ajar, so that as Ellen and Jack approached it, crouching and moving in the shadows, they were able to hear the voices from within.

Jack hugged the wall and moved as close to the window as he dared, but Ellen had a good enough view over his shoulder.

The first thing she saw was Dawson, and a wave of anger rose within her. He had deliberately sent her to her death, without a moment's hesitation. How she would love to erase that relaxed grin from his face.

She did not yet know, however, what he had done with Minna. And her aunt was not in the room. Ken was there, with a gun in his hand, pointed at the moment toward the floor. With them was a big man she did not know, perhaps Ken's chief.

Jack leaned close to her and asked in a whisper, 'That Elliot?' She nodded. Sometime in their progress toward the door he had drawn a gun. He relaxed now, his mind apparently put at ease by the scene inside. He started to put the gun inside his jacket.

'Let's go in and get things straightened out,' he said. He reached for the French door.

She grabbed his hand. 'He's not alone,' she whispered. 'There are two other men here somewhere.'

The gun came back out in a hurry.

His mind was working rapidly. Two other men, not to be seen. It smelled like a trap. Elliot had a confident, relaxed look, as if things were going his way despite immediate appearances. He had almost stepped inside, put himself in the trap as well, instead of outside where he could rescue Nielsen and Parker from it.

He couldn't drag this woman into a shooting fracas, though. Things were apt to get sticky inside that house in the next few minutes. He took her arm and led her to a point along the wall where a brick chimney rose up alongside the house. He shoved her hard into the alcove the chimney formed.

'Stay here,' he ordered her. He did not wait for a reply but dropped into a crouch and began to move swiftly along the house, past the French doors, toward the front. He wanted to find where those two men were before he went inside. It was possible they were at a window on the other side of the house, getting ready to polish off Nielsen and Parker.

Ellen waited until he had disappeared around a corner. Then she darted toward the rear of the house, and the hidden door to the moon garden.

19

In the library, Ken was barely managing to keep his murderous urges under control. He wanted to cross the room and throttle Elliot. Given the opportunity, he knew he could make him talk. There had been other such times, men as dedicated as Elliot, just as clever. He'd gotten the truth out of them. It had been unpleasant, but it had been successful. If Nielsen would only let him handle this his way . . .

'Where are they?' Ken asked. He had asked the same question at least a dozen times.

'I don't know,' Dawson said.

Ken's anger flared. 'Damn it, I want to know where those two women are. Nielsen, leave me alone with him. Give me fifteen minutes, all right?'

'Take it easy,' Nielsen said, sounding perfectly at ease. 'I've called for reinforcements. They'll be here in a few minutes.

We can take this house apart if we have to.'

'And God only knows what's happening to them while we wait.' Ken fixed a threatening gaze on Elliot, who still looked unruffled. 'If anything — anything at all — has happened to Ellen, you'll answer to me personally. You'll wish I'd let you go to trial.'

'My dear fellow,' Dawson said, glancing past Ken at the clock, 'I assure you I am every bit as worried as you are about the two ladies. The elder Miss Miles is a very close friend of mine, and since she arrived the niece and I have become very close as well — you might even say intimate.'

'Easy,' Nielsen warned. Ken had taken a step forward. He put a hand on his young agent's shoulder. He didn't like this setup, and he wished his men would hurry up and get here. Something stunk like hell. For one thing, Elliot kept glancing at the clock. Somehow, time was working to Elliot's advantage. He was stalling them, and Nielsen knew it. But he couldn't very well let Parker throttle him to get the truth out of him . . . could he?

Dawson reached for his inside coat pocket, and Ken's gun snapped up.

'I'm going to have a cigarette,' Dawson said. 'May I?'

'Be my guest,' Nielsen said. Dawson brought out a gold case, opened it, selected a cigarette and lit it.

'As I was saying,' Dawson went on, exhaling a cloud of silvery smoke, 'I've been concerned myself. I don't know how much you know about the young Miss Miles, but you see, she's recently been discharged from a mental institution. A nuthouse, as the expression is.'

'She was in a private hospital,' Ken said.

'And lately she's been behaving a bit irrationally, seeing things that weren't there, little green men and what-all. She and the aunt had a quarrel tonight and now they're both missing. I don't like it, I can tell you.'

Despite his calm exterior, his mind was racing. He didn't like knowing that more men were coming, who could search the place. If he could just throw them off somehow, long enough for his men to take the old lady away. She'd have to be killed, of course, but that fitted in well with the rest of his plans. He'd already arranged for Ellen's suicide. By now she was almost certainly dead. He would arrange for it to look like Ellen had killed her aunt and then taken her own life.

The most important thing, however, was still his assignment, the doomed invasion of Cuba. That would begin in little more than two hours. Whatever happened to him, he could die with a feeling of accomplishment. All he had to do was keep cool for a little longer, keep them here and confused.

'I have an idea,' he said aloud. 'There was some talk of your place earlier, Parker. Why don't we go over there and have a look around.'

'We were there before we came here,' Ken said.

'But did you take time to really look around? She might have left a note somewhere. In the kitchen perhaps, or that dressing room.'

He saw that he had scored a point with his shot in the dark. They hadn't really taken time to look closely around. If he could persuade them of the necessity of a thorough search, get them to go over to the cottage, maybe even without him . . .

★　★　★

The door creaked loudly. Ellen froze, expecting a shout or even worse, but nothing happened. She took a deep breath and slid through the opening into the moon garden.

The garden was empty. If Minna were hidden away somewhere, a prisoner, it would be here, in this secret part of the house. If not in the garden, then surely in the cellar.

The cellar doors were closed. She hesitated for a second or two. She was unarmed, and almost certainly there were two men down there, with guns. And with her aunt.

Well, she thought grimly, lifting the cellar doors wide, I can't just go through the house from place to place, knocking and asking if they're there.

She started down the steps, wishing she

at least had a flashlight. It was as dark as pitch below. She paused, waiting for her eyes to adjust to the darkness. Gradually, shapes came into focus. One of them, only a few feet ahead of her, was a man.

Out of the darkness, Minna's voice suddenly called, 'Whoever's there, it's a trap.'

The second man was at her side. He suddenly put an arm around her.

'Not a sound,' he said into her ear. She felt something cold against her cheek and knew he was holding a gun to her head.

A silence followed. They were listening.

'There's no one with me,' she said. 'They're all in the house.'

The man holding her said, 'Go see.'

That shadow — she could see him more plainly now, sidled past them and went up the steps. He was back in seconds, closing the cellar doors.

'No one there,' he said.

She was shoved forward so hard she almost fell. The light clicked on.

She blinked several times. She saw as her eyesight returned that the two men were the ones Dawson had brought with him from the boat. Both of them held guns. There was no sign of Minna.

'Where is my aunt?' she asked. She was very nearly beyond fear by this time. She had been through so much that now these two armed men, who looked themselves altogether frightened, did not particularly frighten her.

One of them gestured toward the cells in which the slaves had once been held. Ellen went toward them. Minna was just inside one of the unlocked doors, a terrified Pomfret cowering behind her. Minna was disheveled and dirty but her eyes still blazed with spirit.

'Minna,' Ellen said. 'I was so worried about you.'

'Oh, Ellen, my dear,' Minna cried, flinging her arms about her niece. 'I thought I should never see you again.'

The men with the guns came to the cell. Ellen looked from one of them to the other. She had no doubt they were brave enough, but they were frightened now. Guarding an old woman in a damp dark basement was not what they had signed on for.

From somewhere within, Ellen found the detached calm she needed. She put an arm about her aunt's shoulders and started to lead her from the cell, Pomfret shuffling close behind them.

'Don't move,' one of the men snapped, brandishing his weapon.

She gave him a scornful look. 'Surely you don't mean to use that. The house is swarming with government agents. A shot would bring a dozen of them down here, and how would it be for you, with us dead and you two holding the murder weapons?'

The two men looked confused, exchanging glances. One of them said, 'It can't make much difference now. If we're trapped here, we're trapped.'

'But you aren't trapped,' she said evenly. 'Not yet, at least.' She saw the quick flicker of hope in their eyes. 'The garden is empty, you already know that. The door to the outside is open. If you go now, before the men in the house discover the garden, you have a chance of escaping. Even of trying again what you tried to do tonight.'

One of the two looked over his shoulder, at the cellar doors. 'I don't like leaving them here, to sound the alarm.' He lifted his gun.

'You can escape,' Ellen told them coolly, 'or you can have the pleasure of shooting us. One of the other, but you can't hope to do both.'

'Let's go,' one of them said. He slipped his gun into the waistband of his trousers. The other man did likewise and the two of them ran up the steps. They paused at the cellar doors, peering cautiously out. Then they were gone.

Ellen held her breath, hoping they wouldn't think of locking the cellar doors, but they were in too much of a hurry now. Faintly in the distance she heard the creak of the outer door. They were gone.

'Dear child,' Minna said, 'I shall never again think of you as helpless.'

'I don't think I will either. Come on, we've got to go inside.' They went up, emerging into the moonlight.

'Ma'am,' Pomfret said in a tremulous voice.

'It's all right, Pomfret,' Minna said,

'You stay here in the garden. You'll be safe now.'

Ellen thought of Dawson, so relaxed, so confident. She wanted nothing so much as to wipe that smug smile from his face. If only they were still in time. If Dawson hadn't somehow managed to crawl away.

20

'All right,' Nielsen said, ignoring the furious looks Parker was throwing at him like so many poisoned darts, 'we'll go search that cottage, just in case. But you'll come with us, and I warn you against attempting to escape. Because if that happened and Parker came after you, I won't come along to discourage whatever he might do.'

Dawson shrugged. 'It's all the same to me. My only wish is to see both the Misses Miles again, safe and sound.'

They had all turned toward the hall, so they did not see the bookcase slide silently open behind them.

'It isn't often I get to play fairy godmother, and give a person what he wishes for,' Minna said, a touch of wry amusement in her voice.

The three men whirled about. Ellen was watching Dawson, deriving a very nasty sort of pleasure from the shock on his face, and the way all the blood seemed to drain from it.

'You . . . ' he gasped, and went speechless.

Ken was almost as dazed. 'Darling,' he said, letting his hand with the gun fall to his side. Nielsen, for perhaps the second or third time in his life, was surprised too. 'Miss Miles?' he said.

At that moment, Jack stepped into the room from the hall. Seeing Ellen, he said, 'What the hell are you doing here?'

Everyone was startled into immobility. Dawson recovered first. In two quick steps he was across the room and had seized Ellen, flinging her in front of him as a shield. She hadn't even time to step aside before she was in his arms and he had a knife at her throat.

'Ellen,' Ken cried, but it was too late.

Dawson said, 'I'll slit her throat. We're going out through the garden. I warn you, don't try anything.'

He went quickly, not giving them time to consider their options. Ellen came without resisting. They stepped backward into the moon garden and the door swung shut. Dragging her with him, he ran for the outer door, not even seeing Pomfret where he cowered wide-eyed by the cellar doors.

'I ought to kill you right now,' Dawson told her. She had cost him everything, except perhaps his life, if he were lucky.

She threw back her head in defiance. 'Why don't you, then?'

Their eyes met. Something went through her, like an electric shock, as she read the message in his eyes. She had never imagined . . .

He hadn't either, fully, until this moment. His lips curled in a smile, his first genuine one of the evening. 'If I told you why not, you'd only laugh.'

He kissed her, briefly but savagely. Then he had shoved her away and was through the wall. Across the garden, she heard the library door open.

Ken grabbed her, turning her toward him. She felt numb, but she nodded when he asked, 'Are you all right?'

He let her got then and shoved past his chief. 'He's mine,' he said, slamming the outside door open. 'Leave him to me.'

The two men from the boat crouched in the underbrush just above the landing. They had gotten this far, but escape had been only an illusion. They could go no further, not with all those men below, and they couldn't risk returning the way they had come.

One of them counted the men at the landing, his lips moving silently. The other shivered and looked about wildly.

Suddenly there was a crashing in the trees above them. Someone was coming, running hard. Coming after them, there was no doubt in either mind.

'They've caught us,' one of the men cried, springing to his feet.

'Not yet they haven't,' the other said. If he could make it back through the woods, he might yet have a chance.

Someone appeared in the darkness: a man, running straight at them. The man in the bushes raised his gun and fired.

★ ★ ★

Nielsen stayed behind. He couldn't officially condone revenge, but if he didn't actually see it, he wouldn't officially know. Anyway, he had things to consider other than one man, however big that man might have been.

Jack had gone after Ken, but not too closely. Minna rushed from the house in his wake. Nielsen turned to her. 'This invasion, do you know where it's being launched?'

'Yes.' Minna thrust a defiant chin out. 'I've been a fool, I suppose everyone knows that, but that isn't important. You've got to act fast. The invasion is to start anytime now.'

'Where from?'

'A little island offshore.'

Inwardly, Nielsen groaned. There were scores of small islands offshore; it would take forever to search every one of them.

'But it isn't what Dawson said,' Minna was explaining. 'It wasn't for real. It's intended to fail, to discredit — '

'I know,' Nielsen interrupted her.

Shots rang out beyond the wall. Ellen moved toward the door but Nielsen put up a hand to stop her. 'Don't go out there,' he said. So far he had been unarmed but now he drew a revolver from inside his coat, and went to the open door. Ellen saw that, despite his bulk, he moved quickly and gracefully.

'Jack?' he called into the darkness.

Someone yelled from below. Ellen couldn't understand what was said, but Nielsen seemed satisfied. He remained in the doorway. A moment later, a breathless Jack reappeared.

Ellen took a step toward him. 'Is Ken . . . ?'

'He's all right,' Jack said, and to Nielsen, 'Elliot's dead.'

Nielsen frowned. He'd have liked to have had him alive. Still, there were other things to consider. 'This island,' he said to Minna. 'Can you show it to me on a map?'

'If you've got a boat, I can take you right to it.'

'Good. You come with us. You wait here,' he said to Ellen.

He did not wait to see if she did. He was used to his orders being obeyed. In a flash, he and Minna and Jack were gone.

It felt eerie to be standing in the silence of the moon garden. She saw Pomfret across the way, and said, 'It's all right, it's over now.'

A twig snapped outside and she caught her breath, but it was Ken who came out of the darkness.

'Darling,' she cried and ran into his arms. He kissed her brutally, with a hungry desperation.

When they had gotten their breath back, he said, 'I didn't kill him.'

'I'm glad,' she said.

'I didn't have to. A couple of his men were hiding down the path. When he charged at them, they thought he was one of us, apparently, and killed him before they saw who he was.'

She had a quick pang of guilt. It was she who, sending those men out that way, had set the trap for Dawson.

But she quickly thrust that thought aside. Dawson had set the trap for himself, when he had first begun to deal in the lives of the unfortunate men he had duped.

'Those poor men,' she murmured. 'I feel sorry for them. Dawson used them, took advantage of their dreams.'

'Dreams are great things, so long as you keep in touch with reality.'

He kissed her again, more tenderly. Before their lips met, she had a glimpse of the sky above, the color of pewter, and the moon, seemingly lit from within. She had dreamed too, through all her lonely life; and now, here in this once haunted garden of the moon, her dreams had come true.

THE END

We do hope that you have enjoyed reading this large print book.

Did you know that all of our titles are available for purchase?

We publish a wide range of high quality large print books including:
Romances, Mysteries, Classics
General Fiction
Non Fiction and Westerns

Special interest titles available in large print are:
The Little Oxford Dictionary
Music Book, Song Book
Hymn Book, Service Book

Also available from us courtesy of Oxford University Press:
Young Readers' Dictionary
(large print edition)
Young Readers' Thesaurus
(large print edition)

For further information or a free brochure, please contact us at:
Ulverscroft Large Print Books Ltd.,
The Green, Bradgate Road, Anstey,
Leicester, LE7 7FU, England.
Tel: (00 44) **0116 236 4325**
Fax: (00 44) **0116 234 0205**

WREATH FOR A LADY

John Glasby

When Mike Torlin takes on the job of investigating the strange happenings at Pete Donati's carnival ground, he figures it's a straightforward case of somebody wanting to put Donati out of business. Then a peculiar chicken is produced out of an egg: a dead girl, shot with slugs from her own shooting gallery. No killer can sidetrack Mike Torlin for long and get away with it — and when the final showdown comes, he is forced to stand his ground and face up to the killer . . .

MORTAL PROSE

Geraldine Ryan

When a mogul of the literary world is murdered, D.I. Casey Clunes is on the case — though the victim's unpopularity ensures no shortage of suspects . . . Isobel is an intelligent woman . . . except when it comes to her new toyboy. Still, their relationship couldn't harm anyone else — or could it . . . ? The audience gasps as the new portrait of the headmaster of St Martin's is publicly revealed — defaced — followed by news that the headmaster himself has been shot dead by an unknown assailant . . . Three stories of mystery and murder from the pen of Geraldine Ryan.

A CORNISH REVENGE

Rena George

A bleak Cornish clifftop strewn with the derelict remains of old tin mines seems to magazine editor Loveday Ross an odd place for an art class; her artist friend Lawrence Kemp has been acting strangely recently. As Loveday takes the pictures she needs for an article, a grim sight emerges as the tide recedes below. It's the body of a man who, Loveday realises with horror, was deliberately left to drown. But why has the discovery, awful though it is, affected Lawrence and his students so deeply?

BABY BOY BLUE

Marilyn Brahen

In 1944, young Walter Buehl finds his mother stabbed to death on the kitchen floor and his teenage brother Tony crouching beside her, bloody knife in hand. Forty-one years later, Tony escapes from a psychiatric hospital, and a series of murders ensues — with Tony as the main suspect. But Lieutenant Asher Lowenstein isn't convinced of Tony's guilt, and he asks his friend, psychic Tam Westington, to help. As the police conduct a manhunt for the Baby Boy Blue killer, a long-buried truth may surface — at the cost of more lives . . .

BLOOD LINES

Catriona McCuaig

Post-war midwife Maudie Rouse has her hands full tending to the pregnant, sick and injured villagers of Llandyfan, acting as their counsellor, and preparing for changes as the NHS comes into existence — including the possibility of being forced to move away from the people and the job she loves. The call of duty is never far away, even when she tries to steal a private moment with Constable Dick Bryant. Then a fortune-teller is found murdered at the village fête, and Maudie and Dick team up to search for answers . . .

WHEN SHALL I SLEEP AGAIN?

Norman Firth

Eddie Martin is on the run from a mysterious incident in his past. But when he comes to the isolated little midwest town of Garwood, his problems get a whole lot worse. He becomes involved with Sylvia Webster, a young and beautiful — but completely amoral — woman married to Garwood's elderly doctor. Like a spider to a fly, Sylvia sets out to draw Eddie into her web of deceit and personal gratification. Once caught, Eddie becomes trapped in series of murders — a spiraling nightmare that can have only one grim conclusion . . .